M. C. Beaton is the author of the hugely successful Agatha Raisin and Hamish Macbeth series, as well as a quartet of Edwardian murder mysteries featuring heroine Lady Rose Summer, several Regency romance series, and a stand-alone murder mystery, *The Skeleton in the Closet* – all published by Constable & Robinson. She left a full-time career in journalism to turn to writing, and now divides her time between the Cotswolds and Paris. Visit www.mcbeatonbooks.co.uk for more, or follow M. C. Beaton on Twitter: @mc_beaton.

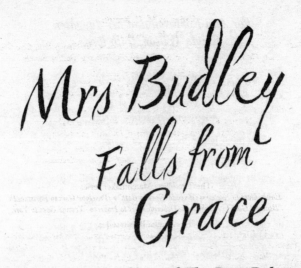

Mrs Budley Falls from Grace

Being the third volume of *The Poor Relation*

M.C. Beaton

For Ann Robinson and her daughter,
Emma Wilson, with love.

Constable & Robinson Ltd.
55–56 Russell Square
London WC1B 4HP
www.constablerobinson.com

First published in the US by St Martin's Press, 1993

First published in the UK by Canvas,
an imprint of Constable & Robinson Ltd., 2013

Copyright © M. C. Beaton, 1993

The right of M. C. Beaton to be identified as the author of this
work has been asserted by her in accordance with the
Copyright, Designs and Patents Act 1988

A copy of the British Library Cataloguing in
Publication Data is available from the British Library

ISBN: 978-1-78033-319-9 (paperback)
ISBN: 978-1-47210-488-5 (ebook)

Typeset by TW Typesetting, Plymouth, Devon

Printed and bound by CPI Group (UK) Ltd, Croydon, CR0 4YY

1 3 5 7 9 10 8 6 4 2

ONE

Ah! people were not half so wild
In former days, when, starchly mild,
Upon her high-heeled Essex smiled
The brave Queen Bess.

W. S. LANDOR

Of the five remaining members of the *ton* who were
owners of the Poor Relation Hotel in Bond Street, Mrs
Eliza Budley was the one least suited to their rackety
life. Despite many setbacks, they had all kept the hotel
afloat with a combination of good luck, good management and thievery.

For the name 'the Poor Relation' was based on their
former lives when they had subsisted on hand-outs
from rich relatives. Before, when funds were low, one
of them had gone out on a thieving expedition. Now
money was low again and they had drawn straws and
Mrs Budley had drawn the short one.

It should have been one of the others, she thought
gloomily. Lady Fortescue, whose home had been
turned into the hotel, although very old and white
haired, was autocratic and had a great deal of courage.
Colonel Sandhurst, although equally elderly, had been

used to fighting wars and to commanding men. Horrible old Sir Philip Sommerville had few morals if any and lifted expensive trifles from his relatives with all the lack of conscience of a jackdaw. And her friend, Miss Letitia Tonks, a thin, faded spinster when she had first arrived to join forces with the other poor relations, had become a stylish and confident lady.

Mrs Budley twisted the short straw in her hands, which the others had left her to contemplate. Although in her early thirties, she looked much younger, a pretty, dainty woman, stylishly gowned with large pansy-brown eyes and a quantity of fluffy brown hair. For the first time in a long time, she wished her hedonistic husband, Jack, were still alive. Jack had gambled away his fortune with great aplomb. *He* would have thought nothing of thieving. But Mrs Budley's relatives had been shocked to learn she had stooped to *trade* and she knew that not one of them would give her house-room. Her heart began to lighten. Straw or no straw, one of the others would have to find a way out of their financial predicament. She would drink a glass of port to fortify herself and then call the others in and tell them that they must make alternative arrangements.

The others were crammed into the small office behind the reception hall and were at that moment discussing Mrs Budley's lack of bottom. 'Bottom', meaning courage and staying power, was much prized during the Regency.

'To be fair,' said Miss Tonks, 'Eliza does not really have anyone to visit. She showed me some quite dreadful letters from her relatives, and all of them in

2

their various nasty ways cast her off. She is a gentle soul and we do not want her to go into a decline with worry.'

'She's a deuced pretty woman,' said Sir Philip, peering above the barrier of his starched cravat like a tortoise looking over a miniature snow-drift.

'And what's that got to do with things?' complained Colonel Sandhurst. 'We aren't putting her out onto the streets to make her living.'

'Wouldn't do much good there anyway,' cackled Sir Philip. 'All she could earn would be a shilling and a glass of rum.'

Lady Fortescue's black eyes rested on him with disfavour. 'You forget, Sir Philip, we are discussing a friend. If, as seems to be the case, Mrs Budley has no relatives she can visit, then one of us will need to make the effort.'

'I have done my bit.' Miss Tonks looked firmly all about. 'Did I not contribute my sister's diamonds? Did I not risk the gallows?'

'That's the trouble with spinsters,' grumbled Sir Philip. 'Always dramatizing themselves.'

'And that's the trouble with dirty old men,' retorted Miss Tonks, 'always sneering and complaining. Well, *you* think of something if you're so clever.'

Sir Philip leaned back in his chair and looked mockingly about him. 'Happens I have,' he said.

'Well, out with it,' demanded Colonel Sandhurst.

'We give her a relative,' said Sir Philip with a grin. 'Harkee! The Marquess of Peterhouse lives in that great castle in Warwickshire–'

'Not Warwick Castle,' interrupted the colonel. 'That's the—'

'I know,' snapped Sir Philip. 'There ain't the one castle in the whole of Warwickshire, damme. His castle is Delcourt. Now this marquess is in his dotage, he's a widower, and he's rich. Mrs Budley sends an express she's arriving and turns up. Says she's his niece. Old boy won't know whether that's true or not, for he evidently don't even know what time of day it is. She stays for a few days, lifts some expensive geegaws and then comes back here. Simple.'

'The servants,' said Lady Fortescue. 'You have forgot the servants. They may know very well she is an impostor.'

'Most of them are as old as their master, and he don't keep a secretary or anyone like that. The servants won't complain about any missing trifles, even if they notice them missing, for with a master like that, they've probably been ruining him for years, and anyway, servants are always afeard of being accused themselves.' His eyes sparkled with malice. 'It's the Queen's House to a Charley's shelter that our lovely Mrs Budley is sitting up there deciding to tell us she can't go anywhere because no one will have her. Let's go and enlighten her.'

Lady Fortescue held up a thin white hand. 'Stay! We have not gone into this thoroughly enough. How did you come by your information, Sir Philip?'

'Over at Limmer's.'

'And what were you doing patronizing a rival hotel?'

'Only popped in to see how they were getting along.

Didn't they help put the fire out when this place went up? I'll tell you how I know. Met the marquess's nephew, Mr George Pym. He was complaining about the old boy's senility. Said when he went on a visit, there was a whole family of counter-jumpers parked in the state bedrooms who had claimed to be kin and weren't. Old marquess wouldn't hear a word against them. So it'll be easy for a fetching little thing like our Mrs Budley to ingratiate herself with the old man. If she plays her cards right, he may even marry her!'

'It does seem waterproof,' said the colonel reluctantly.

'We'll see what Mrs Budley thinks,' said Lady Fortescue.

'You don't ask such as Mrs Budley what she thinks,' cackled Sir Philip. 'You just give her her marching orders.'

'I must say you are a very enterprising gentleman,' remarked Lady Fortescue, and the colonel scowled jealously. He fixed his rather childlike blue eyes steadily on Sir Philip's face. 'Exactly *when* did you come by this information?'

Sir Philip had heard it over a year ago, but he craved Lady Fortescue's admiration and so he said lightly, 'Oh, t'other day.'

Mrs Budley put down her glass of port and looked up nervously as they all filed into the 'staff' sitting room.

'I was just coming to see you,' she said breathlessly. 'My relatives have all cut me off, so I really cannot be of help to you.'

5

'Nonsense.' Sir Philip sat down next to her and patted her hand and Mrs Budley shrank back a little before the onslaught of a powerful cloud of perfume. Sir Philip did not believe in troubling with washing when a deluge of the latest scent on the market did just as well, in his opinion.

'But it's not nonsense,' pleaded Mrs Budley. She looked at Miss Tonks, her friend, for help, but Miss Tonks was suddenly absorbed in pleating the fringes of her shawl.

Sir Philip patted her hand again. 'We are not arguing with that,' he said. 'But I've found a relative for you. The Marquess of Peterhouse.'

'But I don't know any marquesses.'

'You do now. Listen. This marquess is in his dotage. We send you to Delcourt Castle in Warwickshire, his home, and you tell him you're his niece. Settle in and take a look around. Lift something portable cos you ain't a strong lady. Something with gold and gems. Few snuff-boxes, jewelled fans, so on. There was a marchioness once. Find her quarters and see if the lady left anything. I'll get someone to construct a trunk with a false bottom so that if there is a search' – Mrs Budley shrank back in her chair – 'you can have an easy conscience.'

Mrs Budley found her voice. 'This is madness! I cannot go.'

She looked around at the other faces in the lamp-light. Miss Tonks was looking at the floor, Colonel Sandhurst at the ceiling, only Sir Philip and Lady Fortescue regarded her steadily.

6

'I think you should try,' said Lady Fortescue. 'We will hire a travelling carriage for you and send John and Betty along as your servants.' John and Betty, a married couple, had been with Lady Fortescue for years and when the hotel opened had become the personal servants of the poor relations. 'At the first sign of any trouble, John will have instructions to ride back and we will send Sir Philip here to extricate you from any trouble.'

'But it will take days to get to Warwickshire,' moaned Mrs Budley, 'and I could be on my way to the nearest jail before he arrives.'

Lady Fortescue grew suddenly stern. 'We have all done our bit, Mrs Budley. Now it is your turn.'

'You haven't done anything, nor has Colonel Sandhurst,' said Mrs Budley with a rare show of spirit.

'I own this building, or had you forgot? And Colonel Sandhurst is needed here to run things. I could not do without him.'

'Ho, so that's all the thanks I get,' said Sir Philip, bristling up. 'I was the one who stole the goods to get this place started while he sits there like my lady's lap-dog.'

The colonel rose to his feet. 'Name your seconds, sir.'

'Now see what you have done,' whispered Miss Tonks fiercely to Mrs Budley.

'I'll go, I'll go!' shouted Mrs Budley. 'Only don't fight!'

The minute the words were out of her mouth, she regretted them.

The angry atmosphere left the room, the colonel sat

down, everyone beamed at her and then Lady Fortescue said briskly, 'That's settled. Now to the menus. We have a reputation built on the excellence of our food, but Despard has become too profligate in his spending.' Despard was the French cook. Sir Philip, Miss Tonks and Colonel Sandhurst moved closer to Lady Fortescue to study the menus while Mrs Budley sat with her head hanging. It was a nightmare. And yet she owed Lady Fortescue so much. She remembered how Lady Fortescue and Colonel Sandhurst had offered her a home when they had found her crying in Hyde Park because she was beset with debts and duns. It had all been such an adventure. She had companionship and security, but that security had depended on the rest of them providing money by fair means or foul.

She shared a room with Miss Tonks in an apartment next door to the hotel. Perhaps Miss Tonks would listen to her when they were private together.

But Miss Tonks proved stubborn. 'Did I not dress as a highwayman to steal my own sister's diamonds?' she said, forgetting that she had botched the job and Lord Eston had done it for her. 'I was afraid all the time, but I found the courage and I did it! What have you to fear, Eliza? One potty marquess? Either he will accept you or he will send you to the rightabout as soon as he sees you. Besides, you have John and Betty with you. *I* was not given any servants when I went to my sister's. You are very fortunate.'

So Mrs Budley could only hope that the other three would relent in the following days.

But the arrangements for her departure went inexorably on. Even Betty and John, normally a silent pair of servants, showed signs of looking forward to what Mrs Budley overheard them describe as 'a holiday in the country'. Betty was being kitted out to look like a lady's-maid in one of Lady Fortescue's black silk gowns and Sir Philip was out buying a second-hand livery in Monmouth Street for John. Betty was a spare, bent, gypsy-looking woman, and John was squat and burly and totally unlike any other footman Mrs Budley had ever seen. Lady Fortescue and Miss Tonks went through Mrs Budley's wardrobe, picking out the prettiest gowns, 'for even old men can be charmed', as Lady Fortescue put it, just as if, thought Mrs Budley sourly, she were not in her seventies herself.

Mrs Budley was very much a woman of her age, very feminine, timid, believing men were put on this earth to solve all women's problems and take care of them. Men were there to guide and protect the weaker sex. Sir Philip was a horrible old man, but Mrs Budley had expected that Colonel Sandhurst would have been moved by gallantry to protest at her being sent out into the wilds of darkest Warwickshire. But everything that Lady Fortescue did, said or planned was perfect in the eyes of the besotted colonel.

Her timidity made her unable to cry out against this enormous expedition, to voice her fears of ending on the gallows for theft.

And then the day before she was due to depart, she managed to achieve a certain calm. With any luck, this marquess or his servants would say she was no relative and she would be sent away, safe to return unarrested.

If, however, she was accepted, then she would only steal something that she was sure would never, in a hundred years, be missed. If she did not find such an item or items, then she would return and face up to them and say she had failed and let them send someone else. She was not going to meet some ogre but some old man, made silly by age, who might be glad of her company.

So when she was told the following day that the coach was waiting for her, she climbed in followed by the gypsy-like Betty and prepared herself with a certain amount of enforced calm to enjoy the journey, seizing on each little comfort in her mind. She had her own coach, albeit a rented one, so she did not need to worry about dealing with payment for changes of horses at each posting-house. She had John and Betty to take care of her. She had the latest novel from the circulating library in her luggage. Despite the odd appearance of Betty and John, she was a lady with servants.

She smiled bravely to the assembled poor relations, who were standing on the pavement in Bond Street outside the hotel. 'Take care of yourself,' said Colonel Sandhurst. 'You will be fine,' said Lady Fortescue. 'I will be praying for you,' called Miss Tonks, worry over her friend's predicament showing in her gentle sheep-like face for the first time.

The irrepressible Sir Philip thrust a 'shopping list' into her hand, saying that Despard wanted fresh eggs, fish, and any game she could get, along with any vegetables. The coachman cracked his whip and the carriage rolled off.

'We've made a dreadful mistake,' said Miss Tonks, beginning to cry. 'She is so gentle, so defenceless. And you never did send that express to the marquess. You said it will be a surprise for him. But what of the surprise to Eliza?'

'Oh, stow your whids, you dreary watering-pot,' remarked Sir Philip and scuttled back into the hotel before the infuriated Miss Tonks could think of a reply.

Mrs Budley enjoyed the journey. John, behaving more like an army batman than a footman, barked orders at each inn at which they stopped, demanding the best service for 'his mistress'. Betty did not talk much, but took her duties as lady's-maid seriously, making sure Mrs Budley's discarded clothes at each stop were taken down to the kitchens to be sponged and pressed.

Because of their formidable support, Mrs Budley was treated with deference. She grew more cheerful as the coach entered Warwickshire. What harm could come to her? John and Betty would see to everything.

The plan was to arrive at Delcourt Castle in late morning. Mrs Budley thought it would probably be a very small castle, not like Warwick Castle, of which she had read. The autumnal weather, which had been mellow and golden, changed as the castle drew nearer.

Angry ragged clouds scudded across the sky, borne by a chilly wind. Trees bent down in front of them like so many retainers bowing before their approach.

And then the coach turned a bend in the road and slowly drew to a halt. 'Delcourt!' shouted the coach-man.

Mrs Budley opened the carriage door and stepped out into the road.

There ahead lay the castle, towering above a forest of cedars, chestnuts, oaks and limes. It stood on the rocks on the shore of the river Avon, rising to a perpendicular height of two hundred feet above the level of the water.

All Mrs Budley's confidence fled and she crept back into the carriage.

She took out her prayer-book and clutched it tightly as the coach rolled forward. The road was now darkly overshadowed with oaks and the carriage rolled with a heavy dull sound along smooth rock.

The trees finally gave way and a fitful gleam of sunlight shone down. Mrs Budley let down the glass and leaned out. Now the castle was in plain view, tall, black and immense behind its sheltering walls and towers. The coach moved towards a gateway which looked dwarfed and tiny by the immensity of the two black towers on either side of it. There was a dry grassy moat, drained, she was to learn later, by Cromwell's troops looking for treasure. The carriage rolled over the drawbridge and under *two* raised portcullises and into a wide grassy circular area in front of the chapel and the private apartments of the castle.

A butler came out and stood on the steps. Mrs Budley sank back in her seat quickly. The carriage dipped and swayed as John got down from the roof. She dimly heard his voice shouting something and then the carriage door was opened and there was John letting down the steps.

'His lordship is out hunting,' said John, 'but I explained who we were and a room is being prepared for you.'

Mrs Budley allowed herself to be helped down. Her legs felt like jelly. Clouds were racing high ahead across the top of the castle, giving a sickening impression that the great pile was actually movng.

Feeling very small and alone, she walked up the staircase. The butler bowed and then stepped in front of her to lead the way.

She found herself in a great baronial hall with walls fourteen feet thick. Down the centre of the hall was a table long enough to feast trains of vassals. The walls, which were panelled in cedarwood, were hung with lances and maces and spears, and in front of them stood rows of rusting suits of armour. Up by the ceiling fluttered cobweb-thin medieval battle-flags.

'If madam will take a seat by the fire,' said the butler, 'the housekeeper, Mrs Dark, will arrange your quarters.' He turned to John and Betty and said, 'Follow me.'

So Mrs Budley was left alone. The walls were so thick that all sounds of the outside world were silenced. She walked to one of the windows and looked straight down to the river Avon, foaming fifty-five feet below. Then she drew her pelisse more tightly about her and trod along the huge tiled length of the hall floor to the fire which blazed like a funeral pyre from a strange antique grate in the form of a basket. The marble chimney-piece was so high that a man with a tall hat on could easily have walked under it. Huge logs, like tree

13

trunks, crackled, spurted and blazed in the fireplace. In front of the fire stood a fire-screen with a massive heavy gold frame holding a plate of glass so fine it was indistinguishable from the very air. Mrs Budley had never seen anything so wonderful. Everything was on such a gigantic scale that she felt she had wandered into some ogre's castle.

Her thoughts turned to the absent marquess. Out hunting! But such an old and frail man could not possibly hunt. Perhaps he followed the hunt comfortably in his carriage.

A footman in brown-and-gold livery came in carrying a tray with a decanter of wine and a plate of biscuits, which he set on a table next to a huge winged armchair beside the fire. Mrs Budley sat down. Her feet did not touch the ground. She nibbled at a biscuit and wished John and Betty had stayed with her.

There was a huge portrait above the fireplace of a man in the dress of the time of Charles I. He had long curly black hair and a thin wolfish face and the painted eyes seemed to sneer down at the cringing Mrs Budley.

'It's a home like any other,' she told herself fiercely. 'Just a trifle on the large side.'

She stifled a whimper of relief when Betty appeared at the far end of the hall, followed by a tall thin woman with a ring of keys at her waist. They walked down the length of the hall.

'This is the housekeeper, Mrs Dark,' said Betty. 'She will take us to our quarters, madam.'

Mrs Dark, in keeping with this giant castle, was a very tall, gaunt woman with a greyish complexion. She wore an enormous starched cap which ballooned above her head. 'Perhaps,' said Mrs Dark, in a hollow doom-laden voice, 'madam wishes to finish her refreshment.'

'No, no,' gabbled Mrs Budley. No doubt there was a pretty and unintimidating bedchamber waiting for her. No need to be so frightened by this great hall. Halls were hardly ever modernized.

'Very well,' announced Mrs Dark in sepulchral tones. 'Follow me.'

Mrs Budley was to learn later that the entertaining rooms, which stretched out on either side of the hall, extended for three hundred and forty feet. As it was, she felt she had been trudging through one terrifying medieval room after another before they reached a curved stone staircase.

'This,' said Mrs Dark at last, throwing open a door, 'is your apartment, madam.'

Mrs Budley looked wildly round. She found herself in a cedar-panelled sitting room, very dark, with another huge fireplace, piled up with blazing logs. There was a large writing-desk by the window with a massive carved chair like a throne in front of it. In front of the fireplace were two huge armchairs.

'And your bedroom, madam.' The housekeeper opened a connecting door and ushered Mrs Budley into an even darker room, dominated by a four-poster bed of red velvet. Red velvet curtains like dried blood hung by the window. A huge toilet-table held on its greenish marble surface a hand-basin like a bird-bath and a jug of water that would surely take two men to lift.

'Thank you,' said Mrs Budley in a voice as hollow as that of the housekeeper.

'The master dines at four o'clock,' intoned the housekeeper. 'Go directly to the dining room. The dressing-bell is sounded at three. The castle gardens are accounted fine, should you care for a walk.'

'No, I thank you. I shall rest and read,' said Mrs Budley firmly.

When the housekeeper had left and the heavy door had slammed shut behind her, Mrs Budley said to Betty, 'Have you picked up intelligence about the master? Is he very old? Is he really forgetful?'

'I been putting away your duds, madam,' said Betty. 'John, he'll find out sure enough and come here before dinner. It seems this marquess keeps old-fashioned country hours for dinner, and very sensible too, for I don't hold with this new business of eating at midnight,' by which Betty meant seven or eight in the evening.

'You should not say "duds" for clothes, Betty, if you are to appear a real lady's-maid,' said Mrs Budley, thinking with a pang of regret of the frivolous French creature she had once employed when her Jack had been alive and money had seemed plentiful. 'What should I wear? If he is so very old, he has probably poor sight, so I don't suppose it much matters.'

'Got roaring fires all over the place,' said Betty, 'but it don't half get cold away from them. I laid out your grey silk.'

'Not very pretty.'

'Silk's warmer than muslin, and a good Norfolk shawl to go with it.'

16

'Oh, well, I suppose you have the right of it. But that grey is a relic of my half-mourning and I somehow feel that if I looked pretty, I might be braver.'

'You won't look pretty, madam, if you are freezing cold.'

Mrs Budley helped Betty to unpack. They had nearly finished when John came lumbering in. 'Rum go,' he said laconically. 'Close as clams, the servants here. Can't get them to talk about the master. But there's a rare fine kitchen garden, and if you give me that list from Despard, madam, I'll see what I can do.'

'Have you comfortable quarters?' asked Mrs Budley.

'I'm in a little room on the half-landing below you,' said Betty, 'and John's in the attics. We didn't say anything about being married, for real servants ain't married and 'twould look odd.' John and Betty had stayed on with Lady Fortescue in the former days of her poverty for no wages, provided she allowed them to wed.

'I shall feel better when this dinner is over. Did any of the servants query the intelligence that I am supposed to be Lord Peterhouse's niece?'

'Seemed to accept it,' said John. 'You rest easy, madam. Few days is all you need.'

After they had left, Mrs Budley prowled about her quarters. Everything of value was too heavy to lift, from the huge marble clock on the mantelpiece to the enormous alabaster vase in the bedroom. She should really start work right away and ring for the house-keeper and ask for a guided tour. That's what Sir Philip had told her to do. 'Ingratiate yourself with the housekeeper,' he had said. 'Show interest in the kitchens and look bored in the muniments room and don't stare too hard at anything that might be worth taking. And find out where the late marchioness had her apartments.'

But Mrs Budley only wanted to forget about her predicament until dinner-time. She sat down in the throne of a chair by the desk. There was a huge brass ink-pot and a giant sand-shaker and an enormous seal, so quartered that it seemed to have as many segments as a backgammon board. Betty had put the volumes of the novel from the circulating library on the desk.

She opened the first volume and began to read. The novel was very enjoyable and she nearly fell out of her chair with alarm as the sound of the dressing-bell rang through the castle.

A servant with a basket of logs walked in and began to pile up the fire. She retreated to the bedroom to wash and change. Betty appeared and helped her into her clothes and then tried to arrange her hair but Mrs Budley sent her away, saying she was quite capable of arranging her hair herself.

But the minute Betty had gone, she wished she had kept her close, for there were no curling-tongs and she was too shy to ring the bell and ask for some. She brushed her hair and tried to tame it into some semblance of a Roman style but it remained as fine and fluffy as ever. She bound a grey silk cord in it, shaping the cord into a sort of coronet. This took up a great deal of time and she started nervously as a second bell was rung, the dinner-bell.

She waited hopefully for a servant to come and guide her to the dining room, but no one came, so at five past four, she went to the door and let herself out into the corridor, trying to remember if the dining room was one of the ones on the ground floor which she had walked through.

Rooms led to other rooms, staircases to other staircases. She began to feel quite tearful. Of what use was there in sending servants with her if they were never there when needed?

And then a voice behind her, in a dim passage, said, 'Can I be of assistance, madam?'

She gave a little shriek of alarm and swung round. A tall footman stood there.

'Oh, yes, yes,' said Mrs Budley in a voice which, to her horror, trembled. 'I am looking for the dining room.'

'Follow me, madam. His lordship is waiting. His lordship does not like to be kept waiting.'

And with these awful words he strode off, and picking up her silken skirts, Mrs Budley scurried after him.

TWO

There are more matches made up in country houses than in all the west-end London ones put together, – indeed, London is always allowed to be only the cover for finding game in, and the country the place for running it down.

SURTEES

The footman opened a massive door which swung open with a creak and stood aside. Mrs Budley walked into the dining room.

It was huge and shadowy, with a painted ceiling. A long table ran down the middle of it, set with two places, one at either end. A large fire crackled, sending up tongues of flame so that the shadowy room was alive with dancing red light. Like hell, thought Mrs Budley, complete with Satan.

For a wickedly handsome man, who had been seated at the end of the table near the fireplace, had risen as she entered. He had a hard, cold face and large dark hooded eyes and black hair. He was muscular and fit. Here was no doddering old gentleman.

Mrs Budley sank into a low curtsy and made to move forward towards him, but he waved an imperious hand and a footman pulled out a chair for her, the one at the far end.

Mrs Budley sat down, her mind racing. Perhaps this was some genuine relative of the old man.

The butler entered, followed by six footmen, and all began laying dishes on the table. 'Bennet,' said the tall man, and the butler replied, 'My lord?' and Mrs Budley heard nothing of the following exchange because a wave of black fear had just engulfed her. This terrifying man who looked like the devil incarnate must be the marquess. He must be the new marquess. The old man must have died. Now she was more terrified of him than Lady Fortescue, Sir Philip, the colonel and Miss Tonks all rolled into one. Let them shout and berate her. She was making her escape from the castle this very night.

'You are Mrs Budley,' said the marquess, his cold, authoritative voice carrying down the length of the table.

'Yes, my lord.'

'Of which branch of the family?'

'The Cornish Tremaines. Tremaine is my maiden name,' said Mrs Budley.

'Indeed! How very interesting.'

She tried to drink her soup but was too aware of his eyes surveying her and dropped her spoon in her dish.

Not the usual type of woman who pursues me, thought the marquess. The little figure at the other end of the table from him looked ridiculously feminine and frail. The silver-grey of her gown emphasized her pallor and her eyes looked enormous. Not even a very clever trickster, ran his thoughts, or she would appear bolder, more at ease.

Mrs Budley's soup was removed and replaced with a dish of whitebait. She picked at it nervously. Every time she looked down the table, she received a cold assessing stare from those hooded eyes.

The distance between them made any easy conversation impossible. The dishes came and went, the servants padded noiselessly to and fro. Her mind went back to hunt dinners she had attended in her husband's company. Then everyone had been very talkative, usually each guest praising the magnificent country they had ridden over that day, lauding its bottomless brooks, its enormous bullfinches, its terrific stone walls, its flying foxes, and all vowing that a man who could ride with the Quorn could ride over any country in the world.

She had not thought very much of her late husband, for the shock of the financial mess she had found herself in after his death had made her blame him rather than mourn him. But now she missed him terribly and forgot for the moment how his gambling and drunkenness had caused scene after scene.

She regarded this meal as some slow-moving obstacle race with the prize of freedom at the end. When her unfinished pudding was taken away, the covers removed and the fruit, nuts, and decanters placed on the table, she felt her goal was in sight. One glass of wine and then she would rise to her feet, say she would leave him to his port, and retire to her room, where it would be Betty's job to find John and effect a quick escape.

Last obstacle in the race – one glass of port. Raise it

to your lips, she told herself, take several sips, and *now* . . . She got to her feet after setting her glass down on the table. The marquess rose as well. Mrs Budley found her voice. 'Pray excuse me, my lord,' she whispered hoarsely. She cranked up her voice. 'Pray excuse me, my lord. I wish to retire.'

His voice carried clearly and with awful finality to the ears of the shivering Mrs Budley. 'We shall retire together.'

For one startled moment, she thought he was suggesting they go to bed together, but the servants were there and the marquess was holding out his arm.

She walked down the length of the table and placed her cold fingertips on that arm. The butler sprang to open a door and he ushered her through.

It was not a drawing room, but some sort of retiring room. It was quite small, panelled like most of the rooms in cedar-wood, now black with age. Scented beeswax candles lit the scene and a coal-fire of reasonable dimensions burned in a people- rather than giant-sized grate.

He helped her to a chair by the fire and took the facing one. He stretched out his long legs and studied the flames while two footmen carried in the decanters and placed them on a side-table.

'We will serve ourselves,' said the marquess and waved his hand, so that the great ruby ring he wore on one finger blazed with a red light.

The servants retired, the door was closed, and Mrs Budley raised her fan to her face and peered over the top of it with dilated eyes at this fiendish marquess.

'I think we should commence by being honest with each other,' he said. 'I will begin. In the short time since I came into the title, I have been relentlessly pursued by mamas and their daughters. None have been quite so brave as you to date. I thought by avoiding London and staying here until I put my inheritance in order, I should avoid their wiles, but still they come. I was just on the point of seeing if the portcullises could still be made to work so as to banish the matchmaking and the curious when you arrived. As you know, you are no relative of mine.'

Mrs Budley found her voice. 'Of your late uncle, my lord.'

'I am my late uncle's nephew. Same family. No Budleys. No Tremaines. So no more lies, Mrs Budley. Strange. You do not look like an adventuress. I was in the army when news of my inheritance reached me. I had been at the wars since the age of sixteen and had known very little social life. I am, for your information, thirty-three, and, yes, I am unmarried. Some wine, Mrs Budley?'

She nodded her head, hoping to fortify her spirits. The game was up. She could only hope he would not call the constable. But she had as yet committed no major crime. She had not stolen anything. Nor had she used a false name.

He rose and poured her a glass of wine and carried it to her. She accepted it with a mumble of thanks.

'My parents were not wealthy, Mrs Budley,' he went on after resuming his seat, 'largely due to my father's gambling. I have had a hard life in a way. Now I find myself very rich indeed. The late marquess was my mother's brother. He considered in marrying my father that she had married beneath her and so refused to have anything to do with her. So I did not expect to inherit. But here we are, Mrs Budley.' He waved a hand. 'Hardly a welcoming or comfortable establishment. I have already made friends in the neighbourhood, among the men I hunt and fish with. The trouble is all such friendships are marred by such men's marriageable daughters and socially ambitious wives.

'The answer to my immediate problems is to have a wife of my own. As I have never been in love or what I have read love to be, any female of child-bearing years will do. Yet the misses I have met – and believe me, I have met many who have been dragged here by their families – do not please me. They simper and lisp and cry when they leave, as if implying I had led them to believe some warmer connection was in the offing.

'With a wife and children, even such a gloomy and Gothic place as this takes on life and colour. It is a good place for children. The air is healthy and the walks and rides are among the finest in England.'

Mrs Budley found her voice. 'Why are you telling me all this if you believe me to be an impostor?'

She lowered her fan and looked at him, her large eyes wide with appeal, begging for escape.

His eyes raked insolently over her body from the top of her head to her kid-slippered feet. 'I do not know who you are or where you came from,' he said, 'but it will take me only a short time to find out. There is something in your timid effrontery which pleases me.

You are not some cringing young miss being forced into ambitious marital plans by her mother. Are you a widow? I cannot think a married woman would pursue me, although stranger things have happened.'

Mrs Budley nodded dumbly.

'So you see, in my case, a marriage at present would suit me very well. So I am asking you to marry me, Mrs Budley. Unless, of course, I dig up something really unsavoury in your past.'

Mrs Budley stared at him. Then slowly she bent her head forward and began to sob, covering her face with her hands.

He gave an exclamation and came and knelt in front of her and drew her hands away. 'What is this? Tears? Genuine tears? I have offered to marry you, not rape you.'

Mrs Budley scrubbed at her eyes with her handkerchief. The other poor relations would never forgive her. But the time had come to tell the truth. She looked steadily into those hooded black eyes which were on a level with her own and said simply, 'I apologize for having come here on false pretences, my lord. I came to rob you.'

'Of what? My land, my castle, my horses? What, pray?'

She gave a shaky laugh. Now that she was telling the truth, relief flooded her body and made her bold.

'Nothing so grand,' she said. 'Just some very expensive trifle which could be pawned or sold.'

He retreated to his chair and studied her again. 'You could have thieved well enough in the houses of

London, Mrs Budley. I assume you come from London?'

She nodded.

'So? It is an expensive journey to Warwickshire.'

'I will tell you all and throw myself on your mercy,' said Mrs Budley with a pleading movement of her hands which robbed the words of theatricality.

'Have you heard of the Poor Relation Hotel in Bond Street?'

'Someone mentioned it the other day. An odd name.'

'I am part-owner of that hotel.'

'This becomes more fascinating by the minute. What is the part-proprietor of a West End hotel doing travelling far into the country to rob a marquess?'

'It is all that old wretch, Sir Philip's, fault,' said Mrs Budley bitterly. 'Oh, I had better begin at the beginning.

'My husband, Jack, was a gambler and left me destitute. I was sitting in Hyde Park crying my eyes out when I was approached by Lady Fortescue and Colonel Sandhurst. They told me they were poor relations, of the genteel poor, that Lady Fortescue owned a house in Bond Street but little else and that they planned to found a colony of other poor relations so that we might share what we had and in return have each other's company. At the beginning, there were six of us: myself, my friend, Harriet James, Lady Fortescue, Colonel Sandhurst, Sir Philip Sommerville, and Miss Tonks. Sir Philip suggested the idea of the hotel. He said we should call it the Poor Relation and that our relatives would be so outraged they would buy us out. Miss James married the Duke of Rowcester, and that left five of us. Lady Fortescue is now committed to keeping the hotel running, as are the others. We are low in funds. We drew straws. I drew the short one and was told to go and steal something from one of my rich relatives. The fact that all my relatives have cut me off was a cheering one until Sir Philip decided to invent a relative for me, namely you, or rather your uncle. Sir Philip claimed to have had it on the latest intelligence that your uncle was alive, the present marquess, and in his dotage, that he would not know I was not a relative. I was to stay a few days and then lift some expensive trifle.'

'Amazing! What of morals, Mrs. Budley? Do you not fear for your immortal soul?'

'No,' she said. 'Not at all. You do not know what it is like to shift and scrape. I was lucky. I still had food in the larder when they found me. But Colonel Sandhurst fainted in the Park from hunger. That is how Lady Fortescue found *him*. If we have stolen anything previously, and I am not admitting we have, it was trifles which were not missed, and which did not cause pain to the owner. I can only beg you not to betray me.'

There was a long silence, broken only by the crackling of the fire.

It was a silence in which Mrs. Budley suddenly realized what she had done. Not only had she betrayed herself to him but the others as well. She turned quite white and her hand fluttered to her breast.

'I will not betray you on one condition,' he said.

'And that is?' She stared at him as if hypnotized by a snake.

'That you give me a week of your company.'

'Company?' she echoed, thinking it a euphemism for the pleasures of the bedchamber.

'Only company. I have not been in the way of enjoying female company. There is no need to look so frightened. When I say "company", that is all I mean. Then you may return to your odd companions. I should be shocked by you, Mrs Budley, but I find you somewhat endearing. So will you stop looking at me as if I am about to bite you? Relax. Be at ease. I have never coerced an unwilling woman yet into my bed and do not mean to start now. So you may begin to entertain me by telling me about your companions. Let us start with Lady Fortescue.'

'May I have some more wine?'

'By all means.' He rose and filled her glass.

She sipped her wine slowly, glancing at him doubtfully from time to time. But he waited patiently. She was wondering whether to trust him. It was a cruel, harsh face, she decided, and yet somehow she trusted him. She had to trust him!

'Lady Fortescue,' she began, 'is, I believe, in her seventies, a great age, but still agile. The hotel means so much to her, because it means such companionship and comfort.'

'Hardly a success if she must be party to sending an innocent like you out thieving. Go on. Appearance?'

'Tall. Not stooped. Very black eyes like . . .' She bit her lip. She had been about to say, 'Like yours', but

29

decided quickly that was too intimate a remark. 'White hair and wears paint. She used to wear black although her husband has been dead this age, but Colonel Sandhurst, who appears to be in love with her, persuaded her to put off her mourning weeds.'

'How old is this colonel?'

'I overheard Sir Philip say he was probably the same age as Lady Fortescue.'

'You amaze me. For some it seems that love never dies. For me, it never begins. Go on.'

'Colonel Sandhurst has several times showed that he would like to take the profits after the sale of the business and retire to the country with Lady Fortescue. Lady Fortescue is related to the Duke of Rowcester and at first, when he threatened to have her committed, the colonel said she was his affianced bride but I have heard no more talk of a wedding, and then I doubt if Sir Philip Sommerville would allow it.'

'How so?'

'Because he is nutty about Lady Fortescue himself and very jealous of the colonel.'

'What a geriatric triangle! I assume Sir Philip is equally ancient.'

'Oh, yes, but there is no comparison with the colonel. Colonel Sandhurst is a fine-looking gentleman and still handsome. Sir Philip is like a smelly old tortoise.'

'So why do the rest of you tolerate this horrible Sir Philip?'

'Because you need someone ruthless in business,' said Mrs Budley earnestly. 'May I have another glass of wine?'

'Your wish is my command. But do not become too foxed or I will never hear the rest of your tale.' He filled her glass again.

'For example,' went on Mrs Budley, beginning to feel amazingly comfortable, 'a family who stayed with us had a reputation of not paying their bills. Sir Philip said they would probably try to sneak off during the night. So he searched their rooms and found a bag of sovereigns and pushed it down the back of the sofa in their sitting room. They did leave during the night, but Sir Philip had the sovereigns.'

'But what if they *had* paid their bill and accused the hotel of theft?'

'Then they would have been thoroughly embarrassed, for the sovereigns would have been found down the back of the sofa, just as if they had got there by mistake.'

'I am beginning to see the use of Sir Philip. More.'

'Miss Tonks's sister, who is quite a dreadful woman, arrived with her husband to find out if the Miss Tonks, who had been mentioned in the newspapers as one of the owners, was really her sister, but Sir Philip dressed up as Miss Tonks and trounced them.' Mrs Budley gave a rather tipsy giggle.

'So we come to Miss Tonks.'

'Letitia is my friend, although' – here Mrs Budley's face darkened – 'I thought she might have stood by me instead of encouraging the others to send me here. She is a spinster and was very shy when we first started off together, but one cannot remain shy with such as Sir Philip around with his damned insults.' Mrs Budley

31

coloured up and looked down into her wine in surprise, as if it were full of swear-words. 'I do beg your pardon, my lord.'

'You mentioned a Harriet James.'

'Yes, she was our cook when we began, but she married the Duke of Rowcester. She made up her mind to marry him after he rescued her from the hotel after it had been set on fire.'

'Dukes do not usually marry cooks.'

'Harriet was good *ton*, and besides, the duke was once in love with her when she was a debutante.'

'So this fire? Was it an accident?'

'Sir Philip does not think so, for Harriet was locked in her room. Lady Fortescue said it was probably started by some rival hotel, but if that were the case, why lock Harriet in her room?'

'To stop her sounding the alarm?'

'I hadn't thought of that.'

'How old are you?' he asked abruptly.

'I am above thirty.'

'Strange. You look very young. But candlelight is always flattering.'

'When marquesses are not,' countered Mrs Budley tartly and then was amazed at her own temerity.

He smiled. 'You have had a long day and must rest. Tomorrow, if the weather is fine, we will ride out and view the countryside. You do ride?'

'I ride anything,' said Mrs Budley proudly. 'Jack taught me. I used to be so terrified of the horses he threw me up on, and often they just tossed me off their backs. So I had to learn, or I would have been a mass of broken bones.'

'I will find you a pleasant mount. Perhaps you do not rise early?'

'Oh, *very* early.' Mrs Budley got to her feet and stood swaying. She put a hand to her brow. 'I fear I have drunk too much.'

'Come, I will escort you to your quarters.'

He put his hand under her elbow to assist her. They walked together along through a chain of rooms and then up a stone staircase. The marquess held a candle in one hand while supporting her with the other, and crazy dancing shadows fled up the stone walls on either side like so many castle ghosts fleeing at their approach.

Betty was standing waiting silently outside the door to Mrs Budley's apartment. 'Thank you, my lord,' she said, walking forward and taking charge of Mrs Budley. 'I will put madam to bed.'

He bowed and left. Mrs Budley slumped against Betty, who led her into the sitting room. 'He knows all, Betty,' she cried. 'I told him everything.'

'I have never known you to come back from the dinner-table glorious before,' chided Betty. 'You do not know what you are saying. John has just been here to tell me that the old marquess died six months ago. Hush, now. Your nerves and the wine have got the better of you. Of course you didn't tell him the truth.'

'But I did,' wailed Mrs Budley, 'and he asked me to m-marry h-him.'

'This is mortal bad,' said Betty. 'I'll get John.'

She darted out with that girlish sprightliness of hers, odd in such a bent figure.

Mrs Budley sat down by the fire, her head reeling.

Betty returned in a short time with John. Both stood in front of her, their eyes stern.

'Now, madam,' said John. 'Let's be having all of it.'

Sobering rapidly, Mrs Budley said, 'I was overset. He discovered I am an impostor.'

'Not a hanging matter,' said John. 'What else?'

'I told him all about us, about how I had come to r-rob him . . .'

'We'd best be out of here fast,' said John. 'At least he won't know where to find you.'

'H-he does. I told him all about the Poor Relation Hotel and–'

'You had no right to do that there,' said John fiercely. 'Me and Betty belong by rights to Lady Fortescue and all our loyalty is to her.'

'But he will not betray me . . . any of us . . . so long as I stay a few days to keep him company.'

John looked her up and down and his wrath perceptibly cooled. 'There now. When all's said and done it might have been worse. if his lordship only wants a little pleasure with you, then you owe it to her ladyship to grin and bear it. I thought Betty must have got it wrong when she reported you had said his lordship had proposed to you.'

'But he did,' wailed Mrs Budley. 'And I was so overset that I told him the truth!'

'I don't understand,' said Betty crossly. 'You were on the edge of being a marchioness, so you chose to not only betray yourself but my lady as well?'

'Oh, Betty, it is not so bad. Honestly. He said that

34

provided I spend some time in his company – and only his company – that he would keep quiet.'

'And you believed him?' John stood over her, his hands on his hips. Visiting foreign nobles and their families were often appalled at the democratic out-spokenness of the English lower orders to their betters. John addressed Mrs Budley like an equal. 'Well, Mrs Budley, whether his lordship has company or dalliance in mind, it does not matter. It is your duty to protect Lady Fortescue. You will keep his lordship sweet and we will be here to see you do it.'

'Just wait till Sir Philip hears what you've done,' said Betty with gloomy relish.

'Do you have to tell the rest?' pleaded Mrs Budley.

''Tis our duty to do so,' said John. 'What if he changes his mind one day and betrays the lot of us?'

'I shall deny everything,' gasped Mrs Budley. 'I shall say he is lying.'

'Your word against a marquess?' John loomed over her. 'Harkee, the Duke of Rowcester will begin to search through his mansion, remembering Sir Philip's visit, and will discover whatever it was he took, for Sir Philip still hasn't told nobody what he filched. Then there'll be others. You'll have us all at Newgate. No, it's up to you to do your best. That's all I am saying for now.' And having delivered himself of this lecture with all the authority of a cross father, John suddenly remembered his role in life and sketched a bow before taking his leave.

The poor relations were in their sitting room discussing Mrs Budley. Dinner at the hotel was over. It had been a busy day. Several people had left and had paid their bills without having to be threatened or coerced into doing so – an odd event in an age when society took pride in paying as few people as possible – and more people had arrived to take up the empty rooms.

'We should have waited,' said Lady Fortescue, 'and not sent little Mrs Budley off to that castle. There was no need to panic after all over lack of funds. She'll make a mull of it. Those innocent types always do,' remarked Lady Fortescue with all the aplomb of a hardened criminal.

'She'll soon he back,' said Sir Philip and shifted uneasily in his chair. 'Pass the decanter, Colonel.'

'Sinking it a bit tonight, aren't you?' remarked the colonel but he passed the decanter.

'What sort of friend am I?' cried Miss Tonks, striking her flat chest. 'I should have protested. I should have stopped her going.'

Lady Fortescue waited for the inevitable withering remark from Sir Philip, who always slapped down the spinster when she became theatrical, but Sir Philip was staring moodily into his brandy glass, tipping the fiery liquid this way and that. Lady Fortescue's black eyes suddenly narrowed. She rose and picked up an oil lamp and placed it on a table next to Sir Philip and stood studying him.

He gave a shifty smile. 'Admiring my handsome phiz, dear lady?'

'Guilt is emanating from you like a dark cloud, Sir Philip. Instead of helping us at the dinner, you were drinking in Limmer's. No, don't deny it. For the footboy saw you going in there at six.'

'What does that little fart catcher know about anything?' retorted Sir Philip defensively, using the vulgar cant for a foot-boy, who had earned the crude title because he always walked so close behind master or mistress.

'Ladies present,' said the colonel wrathfully.

'Oh, don't mind *me*,' said Miss Tonks. 'The man has a mouth like a common sewer, with rats of vulgarity running around in it.'

Lady Fortescue listened neither to the colonel nor to Miss Tonks. She continued to study Sir Philip.

'Limmer's is where you picked up the gossip about the doddering marquess,' she said. 'You go to Limmer's tonight and come back worried and pensive. Out with it! We may as well know the worst.'

'Peterhouse died six months ago,' said Sir Philip.

There was a shocked silence.

Miss Tonks was the first to find her voice.

'And who is the new marquess?'

'Rupert Lamont Sinclair Bretherton. Aged thirty-three. Soldier. Major in the 49th. Hard as old boots. Bachelor. Don't all stare at me like that. How was I to know?'

'You know what I think?' said the colonel wrathfully. 'I think you got hold of an old piece of gossip and tried to pass it off as new coin. We had better rescue Mrs Budley.'

'Pooh, pooh,' said Sir Philip, relieved now that the worst was out. 'She is probably already on her way back here. He will have told her she is no relative of his. The gossips say that matchmaking mamas have

37

been trudging out to Warwickshire in droves with their charges. He will think she is after him and send her packing. Betty and John are there to protect her. He won't know she meant to thieve. He can only be flattered that such a pretty lady appears to favour him.'

'Have you thought about the *shame* of it?' exclaimed Miss Tonks. 'Poor Eliza. She must be suffering dread-fully!'

THREE

I hate the town, and all its ways;
Ridottos, operas, and plays;
The ball, the ring, the mall, the Court,
Wherever the beau monde *resort;*
Where beauties lie in ambush for folks,
Earl Staffords and the Dukes of Norfolks;

HENRY FIELDING

Mrs Budley rose early. Apart from a dry mouth, she found she was not suffering overmuch from the effects of her drinking the night before. What was alarming her was the marquess's intentions. A man who could no doubt have any woman he wanted would not settle for mere companionship. And yet if he wanted her in his bed, she would need to oblige to make up for having betrayed the others. Her experience of the intimacies of married life had been far from pleasant, and so the idea of a handsome marquess taking her in his arms filled her with nothing more than fear.

Her scared mind rattled into the gloomy future like a runaway coach. She would become pregnant. She would be in disgrace. What if the others cast her off? She would sink to the demi-monde and then, because of her age, very quickly to the streets. A courageous and determined woman, she felt, would take the marquess to the lawyers first and get some sort of financial arrangement hammered out. All she wanted to do was to run away and pretend all this had never happened.

Betty helped her dress, saying colourlessly that my lord was waiting for her in the dining room. At least there wasn't a breakfast room, thought Mrs Budley. She could hardly be expected to engage in bright and flirtatious conversation down the length of that enormous table.

But when she entered the dining room, the table had been pushed to one side and a small round table spread with a white cloth set before the fire.

She had hoped the marquess might seem less formidable in the broad light of day, but in black coat, leather breeches, and top-boots he looked more awe-inspiring than ever. He held out a chair for her and she sat down and raised large scared eyes to his.

He looked down at her with a shadow of impatience in his black eyes. 'If you are to entertain me, Mrs Budley,' he said, 'then you must strive to be more comfortable in my company.' He crossed to the sideboard and said over his shoulder, 'What may I serve you? Kidneys? Ham?'

'I would be more at ease,' said Mrs Budley, 'if there was one chair in this whole household not made for a giant. My feet do not touch the floor. Some toast, if you please. And tea.'

'You should see my town house,' he remarked as he served her. 'My uncle was a huge man, as were his ancestors. I do not think any of the marchionesses of the past had any say in the furnishings. You will observe from some of the portraits in the long gallery that the ladies were all quite small. I thought that perhaps riding might be too strenuous an exercise for you, so I shall take you out in the carriage.'

The butler came in and placed a small pile of morning papers beside his master. 'Excuse me,' he said, and picking one off the top, began to read.

Mrs Budley nibbled her toast and drank her tea.

After some moments, she timidly picked up another newspaper and settled down to read. Normally she only read the social column, but anxious to take her mind away from her predicament, she settled down to study a glowing account of the exploits of the American commodore, Stephen Decatur.

He had managed to escape the British blockade of New York Harbour, totally unaware that peace with the British had already been signed at Ghent. His ship, *The President*, pursued and outnumbered, he was obliged to surrender only to find when he was taken on shore as a prisoner at Bermuda that the peace had been signed and there was therefore no chance of escape or of revenge against the British. But the court exonerated him and praised his courage and seamanship. The people of America evidently felt the same way. When Decatur arrived at New London, the townsmen, who were celebrating Washington's birthday, manned a carriage and towed him through the streets. In New York, the ships' carpenters pledged sixteen hundred days of work to provide Decatur with another frigate to replace the one he had lost.

She moved on from there to strikes in the shipbuilding industry in Tyneside and to poverty in England in general. The writer harked back to Lord Byron's maiden speech in the House three years before: 'I have been in some of the most oppressed provinces in Turkey, but never, under the most despotic of infidel Governments, did I behold such squalid wretchedness as I have seen since my return in the very heart of a Christian country.'

Mrs Budley shivered, remembering the days not so long ago when the shadow of the workhouse had loomed over her. Her relatives had blamed her for marrying Jack, and his relatives blamed her for being a bad influence. She had been glad to cast them off, secure in her new 'family'. And now, by her folly, she had put that very family at risk. She gave a little sigh and looked up to find he was watching her.

'If you have finished,' he said, 'I think you should change into something warmer. I cannot understand why you ladies will consider flimsy muslin suitable dress for all occasions. If you do not yet know the way back to your quarters, you will find a footman stationed outside this door to show you the way. Shall we say half an hour? In the hall? It is an open carriage.'

Glad to escape for however brief a time, Mrs Budley rose and curtsied and scurried out. There was, as promised, the footman, and she followed him back through the castle labyrinth to where Betty was stolidly waiting.

John was with her. 'His lordship has a secretary,' he said gruffly, 'and the gossip in the servants' hall this morning was that this secretary, a Mr Wage, was sent off last night to London with instructions to find out as much about us as possible. We'd best hope it's favourable.'

'There is nothing more he can find out than what I have already told him,' said Mrs Budley, striving for dignity. 'My carriage dress, Betty, and the felt bonnet with the cock feathers and my half-boots.'

Betty did not move. 'And where are we going, madam?'

'*I* am being taken driving by my lord,' said Mrs Budley impatiently. 'No, I am not going to escape. I would not do that.'

'Reckon as you've done enough already,' grumbled Betty, moving towards the bedroom.

Mrs Budley stamped her foot in exasperation. She had never been able to control servants at any time in her past, but the grumpy Betty in such circumstances was too much to bear. 'I will not be spoken to in such a manner,' she said to Betty's retreating back. John sketched a bow and walked out.

Lips primmed in a thin line, Betty efficiently helped Mrs Budley into her clothes. 'May I suggest some paint, madam?' she said. 'We are pale.'

'We are going to stay as bloody white-faced as we feel like staying,' shouted Mrs Budley, and swirling her shawl about her shoulders she stalked out, leaving an open-mouthed Betty staring after her.

It was only when she arrived in the hall, her cheeks still flaming with an angry colour which owed nothing to rouge, that she realized with a little shock of pride that she had actually found her own way there.

The marquess looked approvingly at the diminutive figure in the green velvet carriage dress and the green-and-gold shawl. He led the way out to a smart phaeton pulled by two matched black horses. He helped her in and climbed in himself. The groom stood away from the horses' heads. Mrs Budley looked back. There was no footman, groom, or tiger on the backstrap. No chaperon.

He did not talk as they set off and she contented herself by admiring the countryside, golden in the sleepy September sunshine, a Brueghel landscape of wooded hills and the long silver snake of the Avon.

He drove her first to Leamington, slowing his horses to an amble as he explained that it had been only a sleepy village until a few years ago, when it had become a spa, so that it was now an elegant little town with twelve palace-like inns, four large bath-houses with colonnades and gardens, several libraries, card-, billiard-, concert- and ballrooms, one for every six hundred people, and a host of private houses which had sprung out of the earth like mushrooms and housed only visitors. He said he had no intention of tasting the waters, as the same water was used for drinking and bathing.

The marquess then drove her to a place not far from Leamington and a league from Warwick called Guy's Cliff, and Mrs Budley temporarily lost her fear of him in exploring this oddest of houses. The proprietor was abroad and so they were shown round by the house-keeper. Part of the house was reputed to be as old as Warwick Castle and under it was a deep cavern on the shores of the Avon, where legend had it that Guy of Warwick after many adventures at home and abroad retired to close his life in pious meditation. After two years of searching for him, his wife found him dead in his cave and in despair threw herself down from the rocks into the Avon. In later times a chapel was built into the rock to commemorate this tragic event, and adorned by Henry the Third with a statue of Sir Guy. But during the days of Cromwell it was so mutilated by his troops that it was little more than a shapeless block.

Opposite to the chapel were twelve monks' cells hewn out of the rock, now used as stables. The chapel itself had been recently renovated. A passage led from the chapel to the house. Mrs Budley fell in love with the drawing room. It had such a cheerful, cluttered, home-like air. Pictures adorned the walls, tables were covered with curiosities, and light and graceful furniture had been placed about in agreeable disorder. The drawing room was lit by two long windows. One window stood above a rock which rose perpendicularly from the river. In the middle of the river was a lovely little island, and behind it a grand prospect of luxuriant meadows and beautiful trees, and tucked away in the background, a village half buried in a wood. At a short distance and to one side was a mill which the marquess said was supposed to have been in existence since Norman times.

A little farther off on a woody hill, a high cross marked where Gaveston, the infamous favourite of Edward the Second, was executed by the lords Warwick and Arundel.

The other window looked out onto a perfect contrast: a pretty French garden in which porcelain ornaments and coloured sand mingled their hues with the flowers and terminated in a beautiful alley overshadowed with ivy cut into a pointed arch.

The housekeeper served them a cold collation on a small table set in the window recess overlooking the garden. The marquess chatted about the history of the countryside. He was very much as his ease, somewhat remote, and Mrs Budley, cheered by the food, the pretty surroundings, and by this non-threatening marquess, began to relax so that when he began to ask her about herself, she talked quite naturally. She had not been in love with Jack because it was an arranged marriage, she said. Her family, she added artlessly, were not rich enough to allow her to marry for love.

'But I thought I was very lucky,' said Mrs Budley, 'for Jack was very handsome and very amusing. At first it was quite fun, the balls and parties, the Season.' She bit her lip.

'You can tell me,' he said. 'Your husband is dead.'

'It still seems disloyal. But perhaps because I shall not see you again after this visit, it would help to talk about it. He drank a great deal, sometimes six bottles, but then most men drink like that. But he became . . . coarser. I began to dread his return in the small hours.'

A faint blush rose to her cheeks and her ridiculously long eyelashes dropped to shield her eyes, conjuring up for the marquess by her embarrassed silence a vision of a drunken and demanding husband crashing into her bedchamber.

'What was quite dreadful,' she went on at last, 'was that I began to pray for his death.'

'And so, when he did die, you felt you had wished it?'

'Oh, yes.'

'Very usual,' he said calmly. 'You are not God, Mrs Budley. His time had come.'

'I knew he had been spending all his money and borrowing more,' she said, 'but it still came as a shock when he died and I realized the enormity of the debts. I am so grateful to Lady Fortescue, and yet I have betrayed her to you. Please do keep to your promise.' She faced him bravely. 'I will do anything you wish.'

'Oh, my dearest Mrs Budley,' he said, his eyes glinting with laughter. 'You read too many novels. I am not going to have my wicked way with you. You amuse me, but you have no reason to fear me.'

She looked at him doubtfully. 'You really do mean you only want to share my company for a few days?'

'That is all; my word on it.'

'Oh, my lord!' She smiled at him, a slow, warm smile that lit up her face. 'Now I can be happy and perhaps eat a little more because worry was quite spoiling my appetite.'

In the days that followed, Mrs Budley chattered and laughed and felt young again. Betty and John were obviously puzzled. It was clear to them both that the widow was sleeping alone and they felt she was putting the security of them all at risk by remaining celibate.

Mrs Budley had managed to forget about her

47

predicament. She simply enjoyed the marquess's company and the outings and looked forward to having dinner with him in the evenings, especially as conversation was easy now that they shared the smaller dining-table. But on the fifth day, everything was spoiled for her in a way she dare not voice.

They had been to a fair in Warwick because Mrs Budley had wanted to see the Intelligent Pig and was still in rhapsodies over this gifted animal at the dinner-table. 'I' Faith,' he said, his black eyes dancing, 'I never thought to be jealous of a pig.'

She laughed back, meeting his eyes. And then, out of nowhere, love struck her and she quickly lowered her eyes and felt her heart hammering against her ribs. A sheer burst of pure joy and elation was quickly followed by the depths of misery. Her situation as part hotel owner, *in trade*, had made her unmarriageable. All her ease in his company left her. All she wanted to do was escape before she said or did anything to betray herself.

When she spoke, she was surprised to find her voice sounded quite normal. 'I must return to London tomorrow, my lord. The others will be expecting me.'

She was aware of his eyes on her but could not look up. 'And you returning empty-handed?' he said. 'I suppose you must go, although I have enjoyed our short holiday.' He began to talk about a review of a new play in the newspapers and she was sure afterwards that she must have replied, must have said something, but could not remember anything other than her longing for him, her fear of him, and her desire to escape.

John and Betty heard her news that they were to travel back to London without any comment other than Betty's foreboding remark of, 'Well, her ladyship will have a few words to say to *you* on this matter.'

So Mrs Budley stood like a doll while Betty prepared her for bed and when she was finally alone succumbed to a fit of bitter weeping. She had often had dreams of marrying again, but in her heart of hearts she had always known they were nothing but dreams and no man had ever entered her life to make her regret her situation at the hotel. Now there was the marquess, living in her mind, making her body ache in a way it had never ached for poor Jack.

Heavy-eyed, she made her way down the now familiar passages and staircase of the castle in the morning. He was not there for breakfast and when she asked for him, she was told he was in his study and had requested that he was not to be disturbed.

The butler handed her a letter as she made her dreary way out to the carriage. She took it almost absent-mindedly, her whole being willing the marquess to appear so that she might see him just one more time. But as she climbed into the carriage, the front of the castle remained blank and empty.

The coachman cracked his whip and the carriage dipped and swayed as John scrambled up onto the roof. It was a sunny day: Darkness as the carriage moved out under the two portcullises and then sunlight again, flooding the countryside which was already full of memories for her. She let down the glass and leaned out and watched and watched until battlements, turrets and ramparts had faded from view. Then she sank back in her seat with a sigh and broke the seal of the letter that had been handed to her.

'Dear Mrs Budley,' she read, 'My thanks for your company. I enclose something which I hope will help your finances and keep your nefarious companions from berating you on your return. Yr. Humble and Obedient Servant, Peterhouse.' And there, inside the stiff parchment, was a banker's draft for five thousand pounds.

She looked down at it in dismay. Paid off for services rendered. Paid for having amused one bored aristocrat for a few days.

'What's that?' demanded Betty suddenly from the seat opposite.

'His lordship has generously given me a banker's draft for five thousand pounds,' said Mrs Budley in a colourless voice.

Betty's gypsy face cracked in a smile of pure admiration. 'Why, you clever lady!' she exclaimed, raising her hands. 'Ain't you the slyboots.'

'Betty, I have made allowances to date for your insolence,' said Mrs Budley quietly. 'This payment is because of his lordship's goodness of heart and not because of anything I have done. In future, you will address me with respect.'

'Sorry, madam,' said Betty, looking startled and then contrite.

It was the first time in her life that Mrs Budley had been able to put a servant in her place, but she did not realize this little victory as the miles rolled under the wheels, pulling her away from where her heart lay.

* * *

'The expense of *another* carriage and coachman to Warwickshire,' exclaimed Colonel Sandhurst.

'It must be done,' said Lady Fortescue, leaning on her ebony cane, a sure sign she was distressed, for the cane was normally used for ornament rather than support. 'We should never have sent her. What if she is discovered in the act of taking something?'

'The trouble with people like Mrs Budley,' said Sir Philip acidly, 'is that they have a desire to be found out. No, I had better go, and hang the expense.'

'Tell her we love her and will forgive her whatever happens,' said Miss Tonks, clutching a damp handkerchief.

'If she has endangered any of us, I'll send her to the rightabout,' jeered Sir Philip. 'Do not become mawkish, I pray, Miss Tonks. Eliza Budley has always been the weak link in the chain.'

'Oh, *you*,' said Miss Tonks, exasperated. She crossed to the window of the staff sitting room and stared down into the street. 'We were not all born criminals like you, you know.' Her eyes suddenly focused on a carriage which had just drawn up outside the hotel. She recognized the bonnet on the head of the lady who had just alighted, for it was her own best bonnet which she had lent to Mrs Budley.

She swung round, her eyes shining. 'Eliza is back!'

But her elation was not shared by the others. 'At least she's safe,' grumbled Sir Philip, 'but she will not have anything with her and she will cry and protest and I am too old and tired for scenes.'

51

'Then why keep on creating them?' demanded Miss Tonks with rare waspishness.

The sadness in Mrs Budley's large eyes when she entered the sitting room went straight to Miss Tonks's tender heart and she flew to her friend, crying, 'There now. You are home. That is all that matters. Was it quite dreadful?'

Mrs Budley untied the strings of the borrowed bonnet and let it drop to the floor. She sank down onto the sofa. Miss Tonks joined her after carefully retrieving that precious bonnet, and the others pulled up chairs.

Sir Philip began. 'I made a mistake,' he said gruffly. 'I thought Peterhouse was a senile old fool. How did you fare with the heir?'

'He was very kind,' said Mrs Budley in a low voice. 'He knew almost right away that I was no relative of his late uncle or of his. I . . . I told him why I had come.'

'You WHAT?' Lady Fortescue.

'What a stupid and dangerous thing to do!' Colonel Sandhurst.

'God preserve us all from feather-brained widgeons.' Sir Philip.

'Oh, Eliza, how *could* you?' Miss Tonks.

'He will not betray us,' went on Mrs Budley in the same odd flat voice. 'He promised he would not provided I stayed a few days and entertained him.'

Shocked faces stared at her.

Miss Tonks was the first to find her voice. 'You sacrificed yourself, Eliza. How noble! How brave! Was he very wicked?'

'No, no, it was not like that at all,' said Mrs Budley wearily. 'He was a charming companion, nothing more. This is what he gave me when I left.' She took out the banker's draft and handed it to Lady Fortescue, who studied it through her quizzing-glass and then let out a squawk of surprise. 'It's a draft for *five thousand pounds*!'

Sir Philip snatched it from her and stared at it as if he could not believe his eyes. 'I had better cash this before he changes his mind.' His pale eyes studied the crestfallen figure of Mrs Budley. 'When you ain't in the megrims like you are now,' he said consideringly, 'you are what I would call a fetching piece of goods. So who was your chaperone?'

'Betty.'

'Betty's a servant. Don't count.'

'The housekeeper.'

'Same thing.'

'There was no other lady there.'

Sir Philip slapped his knee. 'Compromised, by George. He'll have to marry you.'

Mrs Budley put her hand up as if to ward off a blow. Lady Fortescue's voice was like ice.

'You old fool,' she said to Sir Philip. 'Peterhouse takes a liking to Mrs Budley, so much so that he entertains her and gives her money. He could have sent her packing. What on earth possessed you to tell him the truth, Mrs Budley?'

'I was frightened and overset,' she said. 'He asked me to marry him and . . . and . . . so I told him.'

'Of all the . . . look here, are you telling us that if you

53

had kept your mouth shut, you could have been a marchioness?' howled Sir Philip.

'No, she could not have been a marchioness,' said Colonel Sandhurst. 'His lawyers and advisers and family would soon have found out about our Mrs Budley and would have told him. No marquess is going to marry anyone in trade. Mind you, Rowcester married our Harriet, but in any case, Mrs Budley told him all.' His eyes widened. 'I assume you only told him you were a partner in this hotel.' He gave a nervous laugh. 'I mean, you would hardly say, "I am come here, my lord, under false pretences. I meant to thieve from you. And it was not only my idea; my partners who are used to thieving told me it was my turn."'

All eyes turned to the widow. 'Something like that,' she said.

'Angels and ministers of grace, defend us!' cried Miss Tonks in a burst of Shakespearian fright. 'The Runners may be on their way here!'

'Oh, tish!' said Sir Philip. 'He don't go handing out thousands if he meant to betray us. What's he like?'

Her eyes clouded over. 'He is tall and handsome and very, v-very k-kind.' And she covered her face with her hands and wept.

'Oh, dear. Poor Eliza,' murmured Lady Fortescue. 'She rose to her feet. 'Miss Tonks, take Mrs Budley next door and give her a hot posset and put her to bed. You have had a difficult time, Mrs Budley. Had Sir Philip not been so behindhand with his gossip, this would never have happened.'

After Miss Tonks had led her weeping friend out, Sir

Philip grumbled, 'What's she going on like a watering-pot for, hey? Playing with our security like that. We should be the ones that are weeping, and weeping with sheer relief, if you ask me.'

'She's in love with him,' said Lady Fortescue harshly, 'and she hasn't a hope of ever becoming anything other than his mistress, and the Mrs Budleys of this world don't become mistresses.'

Sir Philip turned the draft over and over in his hands. 'She'll get over it,' he said heartlessly. 'Nobody ever died of a broken heart.'

'Nobody like you,' said the colonel.

'I say,' said Sir Philip, 'I've been wanting a new pair of boots from Hobb this age.'

'You will not squander that money,' said Lady Fortescue. 'Mrs Budley may be allowed to buy something if she wishes. The rest goes to the hotel.'

'The hotel. The hotel. Always the hotel,' said Sir Philip pettishly. He sank down on one knee in front of Lady Fortescue. 'Sell the place, dear lady, and we will flee the country and live abroad.'

'You old fool,' snapped the colonel. 'We have had enough of your nonsense.' He held out his arm. 'Come, Amelia.'

They moved out of the room. Amelia, thought Sir Philip. He called her Amelia. He pressed his hand over his heart as he got to his feet.

'Indigestion,' he said loudly to the uncaring walls. 'Indigestion! That's all.'

FOUR

Dark was her hair, her hand was white;
Her voice was exquisitely tender;
Her eyes were full of liquid light;
I never saw a waist more slender!
Her every look, her every smile,
Shot right and left a score of arrows;
I thought 'twas Venus from her isle,
And wondered where she'd left her sparrows.

WINTHROP PRAED

In the months following Mrs Budley's departure, the marquess hardly thought of her at all. She had been a pleasant interlude in his normally busy life. The late marquess had neglected the estates, not to mention the fabric of the castle, and he had much to do. A particularly severe winter meant that he was spared visits from young ladies and their mothers claiming that their carriages had mysteriously broken down just outside the castle walls.

It was only when the days began to grow longer and winter loosened its grip that he began to think, not of Mrs Budley, but of the fact that he now craved company and gaiety and that he possessed a town house in London. He travelled up to Town and set architect, builders and decorators to refurbishing the large gloomy mansion in Berkeley Square, with instructions that all had to be ready for the opening of the Season. He made calls on old friends and on the patronesses of Almack's Assembly rooms, for he had decided to find a bride during the Season and everyone knew Almack's was in fact a marriage market.

He was strolling down Bond Street on the day before he planned to return to the country, quite unaware of the burning ambitions and hopes his brief visit to Town had already caused in the breasts of hopeful mamas, when he noticed the Poor Relation Hotel. He stopped for a moment and looked up at it. He wondered whether to call in and ask for her and see how she went on, and then decided it would be a waste of time. Besides, he half regretted his strange generosity. The pretty and shy lady that Mrs Budley was had quite faded from his mind, to be replaced by the memory of an amusing adventuress. He continued on his way to meet a friend at Limmer's, nearly tripping over a small crablike elderly gentleman who had stopped in front of him and was staring up at him.

Sir Philip, for it was he, muttered an apology and then turned and followed the marquess. He had spotted him looking at the hotel and would have paid him no further heed had not one of his drinking cronies, Gully Banks, whispered in his ear in passing, 'That's Peterhouse.'

Very high in the instep, thought Sir Philip. Very grand. He admired the excellent cut of the marquess's coat as he scuttled behind him. Then he looked gloomily down at the mud on his boots as he scraped them on the iron door-scraper outside Limmer's. Despite protests from the others, he had insisted on getting the new boots and had therefore displeased Lady Fortescue, who had called him selfish. So it was partly with a thought of ingratiating himself back into her favour that prompted Sir Philip to follow the marquess into Limmer's. He knew Lady Fortescue was worried about Mrs Budley, who had sunk into a sort of depression and had become listless. Perhaps if he had some news of the marquess, he could raise Mrs Budley's spirits and so get back into Lady Fortescue's good books. For when Lady Fortescue was angry with him, mused Sir Philip bitterly, she spent too much time in Colonel Sandhurst's company. Only the other day, Sir Philip had called her Amelia and she had raised her quizzing-glass and had said sternly, 'You are over-familiar.'

The marquess went into the coffee room and ordered a bottle of wine and the newspapers. Sir Philip hovered in the doorway, wondering how best to start a conversation. As if conscious of his gaze, the marquess lowered the newspaper he had just picked up.

He saw the elderly gentleman he had nearly fallen over in Bond Street. What an old quiz, he thought, taking in the full glory of Sir Philip's best china teeth, which had just been bared in a smile.

In such a hard-drinking age, the marquess was quite accustomed to being stared at by deranged people. He gave the 'poor old man' a slight smile and raised his newspaper again.

He heard the seat opposite him being drawn out and lowered the paper once more. Sir Philip was sitting there, leering horribly, or – as Sir Philip would have described it – wearing his most killing smile.

'My lord,' said Sir Philip, 'I am most honoured to meet you.'

'You cannot claim to have met me, as we have never been introduced,' said the marquess, and up went the newspaper again.

But Sir Philip had been cut by experts. He summoned the waiter, and pointing to the marquess's bottle of wine, asked for another glass. This was too much effrontery for the marquess to take. Down went the newspaper and up went the quizzing-glass. 'I shall have to ask the management to remove you,' said the marquess. 'I do not wish an elderly gentleman like yourself to have the humiliation of being thrown out into the street. Therefore I suggest you take yourself off.'

'I'm paying,' said Sir Philip huffily.

The marquess raised an imperious hand and the manager came hurrying up. 'Now, Sir Philip,' said the manager, 'I've been watching, and it's plain to see his lordship doesn't want to be disturbed. You've got your own hotel. Go and frighten your own customers.'

Hotel? Sir Philip? 'Let him stay,' said the marquess, his eyes sharpening. So this was Sir Philip Sommerville. It could be no other. He remembered Mrs Budley's description, and hard on that came a sharp memory of the real Mrs Budley, very sweet, very warm, very innocent.

'I have heard of you,' said the marquess, 'from Mrs Budley, who was sent like a lamb to the slaughter to my home under false pretences.'

'I only wished to thank you for your generosity,' said Sir Philip.

'My generosity was to Mrs Budley and not to you, Sir Philip. Mrs Budley sent me a most charming letter of thanks. And so how goes Mrs Budley?'

The correct answer to that was, 'Pining for you.' But Sir Philip said heartily, 'As pretty as ever. We need to keep her under guard when the Season begins because our male guests are too apt to be smitten the minute they set eyes on her.'

'She should not be working in such a lowly position,' said the marquess flatly.

Sir Philip spread his hands, small, white, soft, carefully manicured hands without one single liver spot. 'None of us should be in trade. But what would you have us do? Starve?'

'I would have you all lead a correct life and make your profits from your trade and not embroil such innocents as Mrs Budley in schemes to rob.'

'Look at it this way,' said Sir Philip earnestly, motioning the waiter to fill the glasses, 'I did not know you had inherited the title. I thought she would be dealing with some doddering . . . with some ancient gentleman who would not miss a few trifles from the castle.'

'Have you no conscience, sir?'

'None that I can afford.'

'You are old, sir, and so the termination of your life on the gallows would not be too great a tragedy, but

60

think what horror it would be if Mrs Budley were taken by the Runners.'

'It plagues my every waking moment,' said Sir Philip piously. 'I pray to the good Lord above to send our Mrs Budley a husband.'

'Mrs Budley is eminently marriageable. She has put herself out of her class by the nature of her work, but there are many sound merchants in the City who would be glad of such a refined and graceful wife. Ah, Charles, how good to see you.' He introduced his friend, Charles Manderley, who had just arrived, to Sir Philip, and then said pointedly, 'Do not let me detain you, Sir Philip. I am sure you have much to do.'

Sir Philip stood up, but he had not finished with the marquess. 'She'll be available for a call at five o'clock,' he said. 'I'll tell her to expect you.' And he scuttled off as fast as he could.

'Damn!' said the marquess.

Charles Manderley looked curiously at his friend's angry face and then at the top of Sir Philip's tall hat, which could be seen bobbing past the coffee-room window. 'Who was that?' he asked. 'Some high-class pimp?'

'Sir Philip is part-owner of the Poor Relation Hotel. I had occasion to meet one of the lady proprietresses once but had no intention of seeing her again. Now I suppose I shall have to make a call. Anyway, it's good to see you, Charles. It has been an age.'

Charles Manderley was tall and fair and dressed in a sort of messy and casual elegance. His friends said he could achieve the same style as Beau Brummell by having his valet throw his clothes on his back from some distance. He had an unconscious grace of movement and, despite his thirty years, an expression of sweet innocence which belied the fact that he was a womanizer of note, even in an age when womanizing was as respectable a pursuit as fox-hunting.

'No more army days for us,' said Charles with a grin. 'You get your marquessate and castle and my uncle buys me out. I think we deserve some larks, my friend. I am set on a new conquest.'

'Indeed? Do I know her?'

'I should not think so. You have been out of the world too long. Lady Stanton.'

'Marriage at last, hey?'

'One does not marry the Lady Stantons of this world. Tell me about the lady in the hotel. Is she pretty?'

'Very.'

'Oho!'

'No, "ohs" about it. I had, as I said, occasion to meet her once. That is all.'

'She really must want to see you again if she sends that old horror to hunt you down.'

The marquess frowned. Now he once more had a clear picture in his head of what Mrs Budley was really like and he remembered her stories about Sir Philip and he was sure that Sir Philip had made that arrangement unbeknown to Mrs Budley. But she had been a charming creature, delicate and dainty and amusing. He would make a brief call.

'Hullo!' prompted his friend. 'You've gone off into a daze.'

'Just thinking,' he said.

Charles grinned. 'I was thinking about Lady Stanton. Do you think she has me in mind?'

Lady Stanton was thinking about Charles Manderley at that moment. She had met him at a concert the previous week and had found him very attractive. On the other hand, she was still ambitious and was determined that her second marriage should be more successful than her first. After the convenient death of her husband, which had left her a very rich widow, she had enjoyed all the freedom of being a beautiful widow and had had several affairs which she now bitterly regretted. London was a gossip market and she was sure that such men as Charles Manderley viewed her as a likely mistress. She had recently ordered a new wardrobe of clothes. Gone were the transparent gowns. All was of the first stare but highly respectable.

It was not fair. If that slut, Harriet James, nothing more than a cook at that Bond Street hotel, could become the Duchess of Rowcester, then she could surely find a good husband. She twisted this way and that before the long glass. Her hair was as golden as ever and her figure perfect. Men still turned to stare at her when she drove out. She sighed a little. The ladies would soon be arriving for tea. She had chosen a new tack, that of cultivating society matrons to give herself some new respectability. She despised her own sex, preferring the company of men, the opposite sex being easier to manipulate. But these ladies, she found, were excellent gossips and kept her abreast of all the new possibles on the marriage market.

She went down to the drawing room just as they arrived. There was Lady Handon, tall and grim and glacial; Mrs Tykes-Dunne, small and fussy and rouged like a harlot; Mrs Branston, rich and thin and much given to striking Attitudes; and Lady Fremley, quiet and pleasant, the 'good' member of the group, whom they allowed to socialize with them as a sort of memento mori, to remind them that goodness might be a desirable quality in an age when one was likely to drop dead from all sorts of plagues and infections.

As soon as they were settled, they began to talk about the Season to come. With the exception of Lady Stanton, they had daughters of marriageable age and had arrived early in Town to 'nurse the ground', meaning to work to secure invitations for their daughters.

After reciting a list of all the possible men, Lady Handon said, 'Of course, there will be two new arrivals, near middle-aged, but rich. Mr Manderley is one, of course.' The ladies looked slyly at Lady Stanton. They had gossiped among themselves about a possible liaison between Lady Stanton and Charles Manderley after the concert and Lady Handon had said roundly that there was nothing to fear there, that Charles Manderley was hanging out for a mistress. Lady Handon enjoyed the company of Lady Stanton, although she privately damned her as a slut. The fact that Lady Handon permitted her own second footman to pleasure her stringy body every second Friday was beside the point. No one knew about that. Ladies were discreet at all times. Women like Lady Stanton were not, and so the friendship gave Lady Handon a pleasant feeling of superiority, enabling her to pity Lady Stanton for having the misfortune to be beautiful in an overblown sort of way.

Lady Stanton fanned herself slowly. 'I think Mr Manderley has formed a tendre for me.'

'Indeed!' Mrs Tykes-Dunne bristled up. 'Wait till he sets eyes on my Arabella. So *young*, so *fresh*, so unsullied.'

Lady Fremley said quietly after a quick look at the narrowing of Lady Stanton's eyes, 'I am sure it is not Mr Manderley who will set us all by the ears, but the Marquess of Peterhouse.'

'Peterhouse?' Lady Stanton looked puzzled. 'He's in his dotage.'

'She means the new one,' said Mrs Branston. 'Divine. My Jessica has met him and he was fascinated by her.'

'How? Where?' demanded Mrs Tykes-Dunne. 'He is not in Town, is he?'

'He is setting his house in Berkeley Square in order for the Season,' said Lady Fremley, her head bent over a piece of sewing. 'Walls to be knocked down to make larger rooms, new furniture, new paint and wallpaper. He must plan to entertain lavishly.'

'How do you know all this?' demanded Mrs Tykes-Dunne.

'My lady's-maid is friendly with Lord Ager's footman, and Lord Ager has the adjoining house.'

'Pooh! Servants' gossip,' jeered Mrs Tykes-Dunne, privately planning to berate her own maid for being such a dismal source of intelligence. She turned to Mrs Branston. 'Where did you meet him, this marquess?'

Mrs Branston adjusted the feather on her bonnet and smirked. 'As a matter of fact, we were invited to take tea with him.'

'Where?'

'At his castle in Warwickshire.'

'And what took you into Warwickshire?' asked Lady Stanton with dangerous sweetness.

'I'll tell you what took her,' crowed Mrs Tykes-Dunne. 'You told me, Mrs Branston, that you were going to try somehow to effect an introduction to the marquess. So you got your coachman to go to the castle and say the carriage was broken and could shelter be offered until it was ready.'

'Really! What a low trick,' exclaimed Lady Handon, wishing she had thought of it herself. 'Anyway, what was he like?'

'Very handsome,' said Mrs Branston. 'Very commanding presence, and all that was kind and courteous.' She had no intention of telling these ladies that Peterhouse had appeared briefly, bowed, ordered his servants to serve tea and cakes, and then had disappeared, never to appear again.

'I remember my husband saying that Peterhouse and Manderley were in the same regiment and very close friends,' remarked Lady Fremley, planting another neat stitch.

The ladies chattered on. Lady Stanton leaned back

in her chair, her mind busy. She would like to be a marchioness and have a castle in the country and a house in the best part of Town. She would get Manderley to introduce her.

'No, I don't think it's clever of you. I think it's cruel,' Lady Fortescue was saying to a chastened Sir Philip. 'He will come because you left him no option. He will exchange a few words with her and then take his leave and she will be plunged into even more misery. No, I am not going to tell Mrs Budley a thing. You will wait in the hall at five o'clock and when he arrives you will tell him that she is still gone out and not returned.'

'But—'

'No buts. Mrs Budley is beginning to come out of her long depression and I will not have her plunged back into it.'

Sir Philip, feeling like a schoolboy in disgrace, trailed off down to the kitchens where Despard, the French chef, and his assistants were hard at work. Sir Philip drew himself a pint of ale from the barrel in the corner and sat down at the kitchen table, blind to the glares of the chef. He was sure the marquess must have felt a lot more for Mrs Budley than ordinary friendship. Ordinary friendship between a man and a woman was not possible. There was always some sexual element there, however slight. If only he could create some diversion which would mean Lady Fortescue, Colonel Sandhurst and Miss Tonks were kept busy. He sipped his beer and thought hard. And then he looked at the kitchen fire burning brightly in the range which the duke had bought for Harriet in the days when she had been the hotel cook.

He scuttled upstairs and went in search of Mrs Budley. He ran her to earth in one of the bedrooms where she was dusting. 'One of the maids is sick,' she said, 'so Letitia and I are doing our best.'

'I wonder if you could do something for me without telling the others,' said Sir Philip.

She looked at him cautiously. 'It depends on what it is.'

'There is a new scent on sale at the perfumier's in Bond Street called Desire of Paris.' He held out some money. 'I would like you to purchase some for me.'

'Why can't you buy it yourself?'

'Lady Fortescue is always lecturing me about the money I spend on perfume. Go on. Humour an old man. There is something else.'

'Which is?'

'There is some gentleman calling at five o'clock to reserve a table for dinner. Very important. A friend of the Prince Regent. I was not told his name. Goodness! It may even be the Prince Regent himself. I wish to surprise the others but I have business to do. Could you wait for this gentleman in the hall at five o'clock. and then, as soon as you have taken his reservation, could you go out and buy me the scent? Please.'

Mrs Budley gave a little sigh. She had been feeling better of late but she still did not care much what she did. 'Very well,' she said, although a logical part of her mind was wondering why Sir Philip could not leave whatever business it was he had to deal with this client.

'And don't tell the others,' he warned. 'It's to be a surprise. And wear something elegant. You have been neglecting your appearance of late. And no girlish confidences with Miss Tonks.'

A gleam of humour lit up Mrs Budley's normally sad eyes. 'Anything else?'

'No, no, that will do.'

Mrs Budley put it all out of her head until she realized five o'clock was approaching. She went back to her bedroom in the apartment the poor relations had rented next door and changed into a walking gown and fur-lined pelisse.

At a quarter to five, Sir Philip was up on the roof, slithering and sliding and cursing and dislodging slates which fortunately fell on the backyard side rather than into the middle of Bond Street, until he finally clutched the chimney-stack.

From a study of the blueprints, he knew which was the kitchen chimney, and taking an old jacket he had brought with him, he stuffed it hard into the chimney-pot and then made his precarious way back to the skylight. Everyone with the exception of Mrs Budley would, he knew, be in the sitting room.

He burst in, crying, 'Fire! Fire!'

'Where?' demanded the colonel, helping Lady Fortescue to her feet.

'In the kitchen. Down the back stairs. Quickly. We may be able to help put it out.'

Unaware of the uproar in the kitchen, for Sir Philip had urged the others not to ring the alarm bell in case it should prove to be a mere hearth fire, Mrs Budley stood patiently in the hall.

She found she was becoming quite excited at the prospect of meeting this noble stranger, and her very excitement was a sign of her recovery from her infatuation with the marquess. She was beginning to feel as if she had just recovered from a long illness. Spring was in the air and the dusty little gusts blowing in from the street carried a hint of warmth.

The hall was usually a dark place, and so the great chandelier above her head blazed with light as it did every day. It cost a great deal in wax candles, but Sir Philip insisted it was the best advertisement they had and it did make the entrance hall look rich.

She turned to look up at it and heard a voice say tentatively, 'Mrs Budley.'

The Marquess of Peterhouse.

How many times in her dreams had he called to see her? A thousand? And all she could find to say was, 'How do you do?'

'I am well. I–'

A door from the back of the hall opened and Sir Philip appeared like a pantomime demon in a cloud of black smoke.

'My lord!' he cried. 'Take Mrs Budley out. No need for alarm. A small hearth fire.' And with that he darted up the stairs with amazing alacrity for one so old.

'But I was to wait here for someone,' protested Mrs Budley to his retreating back.

The marquess, a hand under her arm, urged her to the door.

70

'Never stay and argue when there is a possibility of fire, Mrs Budley. I do not have my carriage, but we will be very unfashionable and take a hack to Gunter's.'

She was now too dazed by his presence, by his commanding air, to protest, or to think that her duty lay with her colleagues. He hailed a passing hack and helped her in after calling 'Gunter's' to the Jehu on the box.

'Well, Mrs Budley,' he said, 'I am interested to learn how it comes about that when you expected me, you were dressed to go out.'

'I did not know you were coming,' she protested. 'I did not even know you were in Town! Sir Philip said–'

He interrupted her. 'If it has anything to do with Sir Philip, I am sure it is going to be a long and complicated story. We shall soon be at Gunter's and you may tell me there. Nasty things, hacks. You would think this fellow might have changed the straw on the floor.'

A few minutes later and they were at Gunter's, the pastry cook's, in Berkeley Square. He waited until they were seated and had been served with tea and cakes before he said with mock solemnity, 'You may begin.'

'Oh, it is all so confusing,' she sighed. 'Before I begin, do you really think all will be well at the hotel? Perhaps I should really go back ...'

'I am sure Sir Philip arranged everything, including the fire. Go on.'

'Sir Philip said a gentleman was to call at five o'clock and that I was to wait in the hall for him and take his booking. Sir Philip said it was someone, he thought, from the Prince's household. Oh, and after that, I was to go to the perfumier's and buy him scent. *That* did not seem at all odd because he is inordinately fond of scent. So I dressed to go out. And then you arrived. And then the fire.'

'Did you,' he asked after a short pause, 'by any chance tell Sir Philip that I had proposed to you?'

Amazed that she was not blushing, Mrs Budley studied a cream cake with interest and said, 'Yes. Yes, I did. I had to tell them why I had betrayed them and what had overset me.'

'You are not to blame. I think what happened is this. Sir Philip followed me to Limmer's today and insisted on making my acquaintance. When he left, he said he would tell you to expect me at five o'clock and then, like jesting Pilate, did not stay for an answer. I felt honour-bound to call, although I suppose I could have sent a servant to say I was otherwise engaged. Sir Philip then concocts some elaborate lie so that you will be waiting in the hall at precisely the correct time and in your outdoor clothes. I then think he tried to set the hotel on fire.'

'He is mad!' cried Mrs Budley.

'He is ambitious on your behalf.'

Mrs Budley looked at him steadily. 'I said mad, and I mean, mad. I sometimes think Sir Philip does not realize our new social position. Such a thing will not happen again, my lord. Pray tell me now how you go on.'

He told her about the castle and estate, and prompted by her interested questions, began to relax and enjoy himself. He loved the castle and his land, he said. Did she remember the Appletons, the farmer and his family? And yes, she did, for she had met them when she had been driven about his estates, and she asked many questions as to their welfare. He thought with surprise that it was a relief to talk about his concerns. One could not do that even with one's friends, such as Charles Manderley, who would have found it all very boring even if he had known the places and characters on the estate that the marquess described.

'Do you plan to spend the Season in London?' Mrs Budley asked while her treacherous heart begged that he would say yes.

'I am opening up the town house for the Season. It is the correct place to find a bride and I plan to settle down at last.'

Although her face reflected nothing but polite interest, he felt somehow that he should not have said that. 'There should be no difficulty.' Mrs Budley spoke with a calmness she did not at all feel. 'You may take your pick.'

'Let us talk of something else,' he said quickly. 'How goes your business?'

'Very well. We are fully booked for the Season and our dining room is crowded every night. That is why I did not think it at all odd that there was supposed to be some gentleman from the royal household calling to see us. It is very difficult to get a table. Society likes to be served at table by such as Lady Fortescue.'

'And yourself? Do you wait table?'

'No, my lord. I and Miss Tonks act as chambermaids if any of our servants are ill.' She looked across the pastry shop. 'Why, there is Mrs Carley. We made our come-out at the same time.'

The marquess noticed the way that Mrs Carley's eyes rested briefly on Mrs Budley before shifting away.

'The lady does not appear to recognize you.'

'On the contrary, Mrs Carley knows very well who I am. I am become as *unrecognizable* as a member of the demi-monde.'

'Stupid widgeon,' he exclaimed loudly and stared so awfully at Mrs Carley that she turned red and gathered up her belongings to make her escape.

He turned to Mrs Budley and said with unconscious arrogance, 'Surely my presence is enough to establish you socially?'

She gave a gurgle of laughter. 'My lord, Mrs Carley and such like her probably think I am your mistress.'

'Why are you in such a position!' he exclaimed.

'Through poverty,' she said in a matter-of-fact way, 'and through loneliness, as I told you before. My situation often irks me, but I have only to remember what my life was like before Lady Fortescue took me up for gratitude to return. It seems another world now . . . society. I remember my first Season. How easy life seemed then! Pretty gowns and pretty compliments and everything laid out before me on a sunny road. I never noticed the wretches begging in the streets, never thought of essentials such as food and clothing and coals. I was still not quite grown-up, I think, when I met the others. An unhappy marriage does not age one but keeps one young and romantic.' She smiled. 'I grow older by the minute and must remember where my duty lies. Thank you so much for entertaining me, my lord.'

He was as anxious as she to escape. He did not quite know what his feelings were, only that he felt uncomfortable.

For her part, Mrs Budley was feeling strangely calm. Seeing him again had knocked all her dreams right out of her head. To accept her situation in the social scheme of things and put aside dreams of romance and marriage meant a certain degree of contentment. She was anxious to be gone.

'I would rather walk,' she said outside Gunter's. 'No, please, it is only a short distance. May I thank you for all your kindness? I shall never forget it.' She swept him a curtsy. 'Good day, my lord. We shall not meet again.'

He stood, feeling strangely lost, watching her gallant little figure turn the corner of Berkeley Square.

'Why, my lord! We meet again.'

The words seemed a parody of Mrs Budley's farewell and he swung round angrily. Mrs Branston was standing there with her daughter Jessica. Jessica simpered horribly. But Jessica was a debutante and this was what he was going to meet during the Season. He glanced over his shoulder, almost as if he were hoping to see Mrs Budley return, but she had marched out of his life and left him feeling a trifle shabby although he did not know why.

FIVE

Like a dog he hunts in dreams,
and thou art staring at the wall,
Where the dying night-lamp flickers,
and the shadows rise and fall.

ALFRED, LORD TENNYSON

The mysterious fire in the kitchen was out, Sir Philip having scrambled back over the tiles to remove the old jacket from the chimney. But the walls of the kitchen were soot-blackened and would need to be scrubbed and lime-washed.

'Most unlike our Mrs Budley to disappear during all the fuss,' said Lady Fortescue. She gave Sir Philip a hard look. 'I suppose you haven't been up to anything?'

'I?' Sir Philip looked the picture of innocence. 'My dear lady, your word is my command.'

At that moment, the door of their private sitting room opened and Mrs Budley entered.

'Where have you been, Eliza?' demanded Miss Tonks.

Sir Philip, who was standing, moved behind Lady Fortescue's chair and winked horribly. 'I have been out walking,' said Mrs Budley, deciding not to betray Sir

76

Philip, for she felt his interference in her life had proved beneficial. Seeing the marquess again had put an end to her silly dreams.

'We had a most peculiar fire.' Lady Fortescue twisted her head. 'What are you doing back there, Sir Philip? Come round where I can see you. Yes, a *most* peculiar fire. Black smoke started coming from the kitchen range. Despard threw buckets of water in it to put it out. We sent for the sweep and he is busy cleaning the chimney, although it was swept only two months ago. Despard is having to manage his sauces and concoctions on a spirit stove and you can imagine is none too pleased. Still, the drama is over. Your walk must have done you good, Mrs Budley. You are looking more relaxed in spirit than you have been this age.'

Mrs Budley nodded quietly and sat down next to Miss Tonks.

'Now,' went on Lady Fortescue, 'in the middle of all this fuss, we nonetheless have some excellent news. Have any of you heard of Mr Hitchcock?'

'Of course.' Sir Philip looked contemptuous. 'Who has not?'

'*I* have not,' said Miss Tonks, tossing her head so that the streamers on her cap swung from side to side.

'Well, that doesn't surprise me. Mr Hitchcock is the rich nabob who is recently arrived back from India and plans to star at the Season. He – fortunately for us – married a rather pushy and vulgar lady, the sort who don't take at the Season here and so are shipped out to India in the hope that some homesick fool will fall for them. Mrs Hitchcock plans to throw money at the *ton* to ingratiate herself and so they are holding a ball one week before the Season begins. They have leased the Earl of Dunster's town house in Grosvenor Square.'

'So how does this concern us?' demanded Miss Tonks.

'Mrs Hitchcock has heard of the glories of our *cuisine*. So we are to prepare the supper for the opening ball and she wishes us to be there as servants.'

'But we have maids and waiters we can supply,' protested Miss Tonks.

'We are the lure, and for our distinguished presence behind the food, Hitchcock, urged on by his wife, is prepared to pay a fortune.'

'But who will take charge here that evening?' asked Mrs Budley.

'Nearly all our guests will be present at the ball, and the underchef can cope with those who are not.'

'It will be,' said Mrs Budley slowly, 'rather humiliating.'

'But the colonel and I wait table here,' pointed out Lady Fortescue.

'That is different.' Mrs Budley wrinkled her brow. 'This is our business here, and society regards it as an amusingly well-run folly. I know some even believe we are only doing it for our amusement. But to appear as servants in someone's house . . .'

'Pooh! Pooh!' jeered Sir Philip. 'How nice! How too terribly nice, Mrs Budley. Believe me, considering what the Hitchcocks are paying, I would serve stark-naked if that were required.'

Everyone's eyes promptly slid away from Sir Philip,

as if a mental picture of that elderly gentleman unclothed was just too hard to bear.

'I appreciate your sensitivities,' said Lady Fortescue, 'but we suffered much, dear Mrs Budley, after we had sent such an innocent as yourself off on a thieving raid. We have decided that in future all money that we gain will be come by honestly.'

'In that case,' said Mrs Budley, 'would it not be a good idea to send Lord Peterhouse his money?'

'Tish, child! That was a present.'

While the others discussed the coming event at the Hitchcocks's, Mrs Budley wondered whether they would have to wear livery of some sort, and whether the marquess would be there. She was over that nonsense, and yet ... For him to actually see her performing such a menial office!

She shook her head angrily. What did it matter if he did see her? He knew what she did. But then, why could she not help hoping that the others might decide to leave her behind to run the hotel?

A few days later the marquess was back in his castle among a smell of paint and decorating. He thought briefly of Mrs Budley. It would have been fun to have her with him, to advise and choose colours. But that duty would soon be taken over by a wife. He did not look forward to the choosing of one with much enthusiasm. An aristocratic marriage was a business partnership. He needed someone of wealth and manners who would share his interests.

And yet Mrs Budley kept creeping back into his

mind. He visited the Appletons when he was out round his estates and Mrs Appleton, the farmer's wife, had no sooner served him with a glass of elderberry wine that she asked him if he had seen Mrs Budley.

'I took tea with her in London,' said the marquess. And how dainty and pretty she had seemed, ran his thoughts. How dare that Carley female cut her!

'I would like a recipe for seed-cake from her, my lord,' said Mrs Appleton. 'I wonder if I might prevail on you to ask her for it when you are next in Town. Mrs Budley said she resided in London.'

'Yes, I will,' he said almost absent-mindedly, thinking of the way she had said she would not see him again. Still, there could be no harm in calling in at that hotel.

'And Mrs Batty over at Tamen said that when she was poorly and Mrs Budley called with your lordship, Mrs Budley was gracious enough to brew up a posset which did wonders. Could your lordship by any chance . . . ?'

'Certainly.' And so it went on. Everywhere on his land, there seemed to be some tenant who remembered Mrs Budley for her kindness and interest. He realized with surprise that although he had entertained a few visitors since then, the latest being Charles Manderley, that he had taken none of them on the rounds, nor had any of them shown any desire to meet any of the cottagers or farmers.

He frowned slightly. His wife, when he found her, would need to possess some of that warmth and charity which came so naturally to Mrs Budley.

He dreamt of her that night. She was running away

from him through the shadowy rooms of the castle and he could not seem to catch her.

Mrs Budley awoke with a cry. The marquess had been chasing her along one of the corridors of the hotel and she had been weeping and crying in her dream that it was no good, his catching her, because he would not know what to do with her.

Miss Tonks's voice came from the next pillow. 'What ails you, Eliza? Can't you sleep?'

'I saw him,' said Mrs Budley, overcome with a longing to speak about him.

'The marquess? When? Where?'

'I was going out on my walk,' said Mrs Budley, still determined not to betray Sir Philip, 'when I met him and he took me to tea at Gunter's.'

'How romantic!'

'Not romantic at all. It was as well I did meet him again. I realized how silly my dreams were.'

Miss Tonks gave a little sigh. 'Because of my sad lack of looks, Eliza, I am constrained to be sensible. But I have often thought in your case that you have every right to dream. He thought so highly of your company that he enjoyed your staying with him and then gave you that munificent draft.'

'Letitia, he is to attend the Season to find a bride and it could not be made more clear that that bride is not I.'

'He has not come to his senses, that is all,' said Miss Tonks loyally. 'He is a mature and intelligent man.'

'Mature and intelligent men want silly, fluffy little ladies, not widows.'

'But *you* are silly and fluffy and I envy you for it,' cried Miss Tonks and then bit her lip as Mrs Budley said in a stifled voice, 'If you please, Letitia, I wish to sleep.'

The next day Lady Stanton summoned her most faithful beau, Mr Jasper Brackley. She had no interest in marrying him. He did not have a title, and he was only moderately rich, but he was useful when she needed an escort.

'The dreadful Hitchcocks are giving this massive ball before the beginning of the Season,' she said. 'Everyone is going.'

'Everyone, I assume, means Charles Manderley as well,' he remarked sourly, being well aware of Lady Stanton's latest interest.

'Yes,' she said airily, not wishing to tell him that she had wanted to ask Charles to escort her but he had gone into Warwickshire to stay with Peterhouse. 'At least, I assume he has been invited along with everyone else who is anyone. You will be my escort, of course.'

'Of course,' he echoed in a hollow voice, wishing he had the courage to tell her to go to the devil. 'I heard an interesting piece of gossip. You know that the Hitchcocks have engaged Neil Gow's band?'

Lady Stanton looked at him contemptuously. Everyone, including Almack's, engaged Neil Gow's band.

'But there is more. The Poor Relation is to do the catering.'

Her beautiful eyes narrowed. She well remembered that hotel and the staff who had so humiliated her when she was chasing the Duke of Rowcester. 'The cooking only, I assume,' she said. 'Never say that the great Lady Fortescue has agreed to appear outside her own domain in the role of servant.'

'All of them,' he said, satisfied he had her interest.

'Then I must certainly be there.' Her lips curled in a smile. 'It is time society saw that lot in their true colours – a group of nasty little tradespeople.'

Although, thanks to their success, the owners of the Poor Relation were used to their hotel being full the year round, each Season, with its sudden burst of frenetic activity, always came as a surprise. In fact, the rush and fuss started at least three weeks before the Season actually began. The guests were grander and more demanding. It was during and just before each Season that Lady Fortescue and Colonel Sandhurst felt the weight of their years. The colonel had pains in his legs and Lady Fortescue found that she craved sleep, even in the middle of the day, and would sometimes sit down on a chair in the little office off the hall and fall neatly and quietly asleep, sitting bolt upright. Sir Philip, by virtue of having led a totally dissipated life, was used to feeling mildly ill and would have wondered what was the matter had he risen one morning feeling a whole man. It was during the Season that Miss Tonks felt herself returning to her former timid and faded image. When the maids and waiters could not cope with the demands, she flew from room to room herself, well aware that most of the distinguished guests, despite her silk dress and crisp muslin cap, saw her as just another servant. Only Mrs Budley was glad of the work to keep thought at bay. For that evening at the Hitchcocks's loomed on the horizon of her mind like a great dark cloud. Despard could hardly cope with the day-to-day meals, so great was his ambition to shine at the Hitchcocks's. He spent hours rehearsing for the great event by producing elaborate dishes, pronouncing himself dissatisfied with the results and refusing to serve them in the dining room until Sir Philip was sent down to read him a lecture on extravagance.

It was some small comfort to Mrs Budley to learn that they were to go dressed in their best, as if they were the guests and not the servants. In the little spare time they had, she and Miss Tonks pored over fashion-plates and stitched and sewed to try to produce gowns of suitable magnificence. Sir Philip had persuaded the famous jeweller, Hamlet, that the poor relations would be an excellent show-case for his wares, on the understanding that two armed footmen would guard them at all times.

Sir Philip's suggestion that he should get some crooked jeweller to produce excellent paste imitations of the gems was turned down by the others. Any further crimes were out of the question. From now on what money they received would be through their own hard work.

Lady Fortescue was blossoming out in full colour for the evening instead of wearing her usual half-mourning. She was to wear a gown of violet lutestring with a long train and embellished on the bodice with pearl embroidery. Ostrich feathers on a diamond-and-gold

84

circlet were to decorate her hair, and a fine borrowed necklace, an unusual combination of pearls and diamonds, her neck.

Miss Tonks was shivering with excitement at the prospect of appearing in gold silk and a real diamond tiara. Mrs Budley had fashioned a pretty gown of figured jaconet with puffed sleeves and a low-cut neckline. From the jeweller's selection, she chose a garnet necklace and had made dark-crimson silk flowers for her hair.

Sir Philip was to sport an even more extraordinary wig than usual, having talked the wig-maker into lending him one for the evening. It was dead-black and made him look quite sinister. Despite the iniquitous flour tax, the colonel was to wear his thick hair powdered, deaf to the gibes of Sir Philip, who said that as the colonel's hair was white anyway, powdering it was a waste of time.

Rumours about the lavishness of the ball spread about the West End of London. There was to be a fountain spouting champagne, there were to be rich presents for each guest. The walls were to be draped with the finest silk. The dishes were of solid gold. Some members of society who had refused invitations began to change their minds and send acceptances instead, saying that their maids or secretaries had sent refusals by mistake.

Staff had to be left to run the hotel, but other servants were hired to assist the poor relations in their duties at the Hitchcocks's. The Hitchcocks were paying so much that they could afford that luxury.

They arrived at the Hitchcocks's early on the morning of the great day. Lady Fortescue was as stiff as a ramrod, determined not to be humiliated by the vulgar Mrs Hitchcock. But Mrs Hitchcock was up and about just as early as they, and her appearance and manner came as a surprise. She was much younger than they had expected, being in her late twenties, and she looked like a country girl: apple cheeks, strong curly hair, strong squat body, small twinkling grey eyes.

'We shall all have a fortifying dish of bohea,' were her first words, 'and then get down to the business of the day.' Mrs Budley sat down gingerly and looked about her in awe. Everything was so richly appointed, from the modern furniture to the heavy brocade curtains to the painted ceilings and marble statuary. One would think the Hitchcocks had returned from the Grand Tour rather than from India. She was to learn later that the Hitchcocks had placed all the Earl of Dunster's furniture, hangings and ornaments in storage and then proceeded to buy their own statuary from impoverished aristocrats eager to sell, along with fine paintings and china. Everything was admittedly a little *too* studied and formal, but Mrs Hitchcock – or her adviser's – taste was excellent.

The poor relations were wearing what they described as their 'working' clothes, by which they meant their oldest, their evening clothes having been brought along in trunks, and the borrowed jewellery to be delivered later, under the guard of the two footmen. Mrs Budley felt they looked like a bunch of shabby refugees from some war as they sat sipping tea among all the magnificence. She could see Sir Philip's eyes darting this way and that, coming to rest occasionally on some expensive ornament, and hoped he was not thinking of filling his pockets.

Mrs Hitchcock asked Lady Fortescue about the hotel and how she had thought of such an idea, and Lady Fortescue said that she had often wanted to go into business and left it at that. No story of poverty.

After they had finished drinking tea, Mrs Hitchcock led them through a huge ballroom at the back of the house to the supper room adjoining it where men staggered this way and that under the weight of palm-trees and hothouse flowers.

Mrs Hitchcock spread out a plan on a table. 'Supper will be at midnight. But before then, people will be coming and going for refreshment. There will be one long table along the wall for the food, and on the other wall, a table with the punch-bowl, the lemonade, the negus and the wine. Champagne will be available from that fountain in the middle of the room.' They all looked solemnly at a swathed object.

'Won't the champagne lose its fizz in a fountain?' asked Sir Philip.

'A little. But a necessary extravagance, I feel. I am making my social debut as a matron and see no reason to spoil things with senseless economies. Place cards on the dining-tables are essential, for there will be gifts for each guest, mostly the same thing, but with the exception of more expensive trifles for the more notable guests.'

'What are the presents?' asked Sir Philip.

'An enamel snuff-box for the gentlemen and a painted fan on ivory sticks for the ladies. As you will notice, Lady Fortescue, there is a stair from the back of the supper room which leads directly to the kitchens. You know your duties? Who will carve?'

'Colonel Sandhurst here,' said Lady Fortescue. 'Apart from that, our servants and yours will help to serve the guests and we ourselves will deliver the plates to the tables. Sir Philip will go around with the wine, as will Miss Tonks.'

'Very good. Ah, here is my husband.' She introduced them all round and they in turn looked curiously at the nabob. He was older than his wife, in his forties, tanned to a mahogany colour, small and spare in stature, and dull of eye, as if uninterested in anything his wife chose to do. He accorded them all a brief bow and then said in a raspy whisper that he thought he might retire again to bed.

After he had left, his wife made no reference to him. It was as if Mr Hitchcock did not exist.

'I am sure you will ascertain that all glasses are of the right shape and do not have a single smear or speck on them,' said Mrs Hitchcock.

'Nothing will go wrong,' said Lady Fortescue firmly. 'Nothing can go wrong. It is your first social event in London, Mrs Hitchcock, and it is our first engagement outside our hotel, so we are as interested in success as you are yourself.'

Mrs Budley had thought that with such an army of servants there would be little for them all to do except supervise, but the preparations were so lavish that they found they had to work as hard as their servants. Despard was sweating in the kitchens, his white and twisted face hovering over steaming pots like a demon, while Lady Fortescue and the colonel sipped and tasted. 'He has excelled himself,' whispered Lady Fortescue to the colonel.

'Don't tell him,' muttered the colonel, 'or he'll ask for more wages.'

Lady Stanton, too, arose early. Normally, as she had the Marquess of Peterhouse in her sights, she would have slept late in order to be completely fresh and rested for the ball. She had met Charles Manderley at the opera the night before and he had told her that he and the marquess would be there. She planned to look her best and see if she could snare him. But she had a plan other than trapping the marquess, and that was revenge on the poor relations.

So she was in her still room brewing up an infusion of senna pods. She intended to introduce the resulting concoction into some part of the menu. The guests would cry poisoning and the staff of that hotel would be ruined.

She had sent one of her footmen round to the Hitchcocks with the present of a box of chocolates for Mrs Hitchcock. When there, he had his instructions to visit the kitchens and find out what was on the menu.

She looked up from her efforts as her butler appeared in the door of the still room. 'Jack, the second footman, has returned, my lady,' he said.

'Send him in here,' she ordered curtly.

Soon the footman was standing at her elbow. 'You found out what I wanted?' she asked.

'Yes, my lady. I have a list here. I memorized it and then wrote it down as soon as I had left the house.'

'Very well. I have a further job for you.' She carefully poured the brew into a blue glass bottle. Then she scanned the list. 'Ah, turtle soup, the very thing. I want you to take this bottle and return to the Hitchcocks this evening. You got to know some of the servants there?'

'Yes, my lady.'

'Then you will accompany me. As soon as I am at the ball, you will go back to the kitchens and try to introduce the contents of this bottle into the soup. You will earn five guineas for your trouble.'

The footman caught his breath. Five guineas was a magnificent sum. She fished in the pocket of the long apron she wore. 'Here is a crown for you for this morning's trouble. You will not fail me?'

'No, my lady.'

She stoppered the bottle and handed it to him. 'See you do not.'

The footman, Jack, gave her a dog-like worshipping look and she gave him a slight smile of approval. 'You may take the rest of the day off.'

Jack, puffed up with the importance of his mission, made his way out to the London streets. Free time was a luxury. Legitimate free time, that was. Footmen spent a great part of their days in nervous idleness, because their role was more ornamental than functional, waiting for their master or mistress to summon them, and that involved hanging about the hall or the kitchens. To be at liberty and out in the London streets was like being out of prison. The day was sunny and mild, with a stiff breeze to blow away the pall of smoke and the smells of the London streets. He squared his shoulders and strode purposefully in the direction of the Running Footman, a pub much frequented by servants, just off Berkeley Square. He was a tall, handsome young man, lately come up from the country, and his height and looks had quickly secured him a position. In his plush livery, he appeared an imposing figure but inside his head there still lived a country boy, and his mind still gawped at the wonders of the Town although his face had already become permanently set in what he considered an awe-inspiring sneer.

The tavern was crowded although it was still morning, for that was when the other footmen were supposed to be about their duties, delivering cards from masters who did not wish to call in person on the misses they had danced with the night before, gilt-edged invitations, flowers, poems and gifts. And so they each took the opportunity to drop in to the Running Footman to meet their cronies.

The first remark that greeted Jack caught him on the raw. 'Here's our bumpkin,' cried Lord Ritcher's footman, a tall, thin man who was jealous of young newcomers to the footman scene.

Jack subsided languidly into a chair opposite. 'Bumpkin yourself,' he drawled in a Londonized voice through which patches of country burr still surfaced like dark patches on a badly powdered footman's head. 'I am out on a secret mission.'

Another, kinder, footman laughed indulgently. 'You'll get used to those secret missions, my friend. My lady wishes to set up a flirt, that is all, but they go on about it as if one were carrying secrets to the French.'

Jack shrugged and called for a pint of shrub. 'Nothing like that, no,' he said languidly. 'Certainly it is more in the line of carrying secrets to the French.'

A butler who had been passing their table heard this and stopped short. 'Hey, young fellow, if you are playing traitor, I'll have you in the Tower.'

'No,' said Jack, alarmed. 'Nothing like that. Englishman to the bone, that's me.'

'In other words, even his brain-box is English,' sneered Lord Richter's footman.

Jack relapsed into a sulky silence, but the curiosity of the others at his table had been well and truly whetted and their curiosity spread to the other patrons of the Running Footman. Soon Jack was being plied with drinks. He was sharp enough to know the reason for this generous hospitality, and although he felt a trifle unsteady on his legs when he left, he congratulated himself that he had kept his mouth shut and went back to put his head under the pump and to drink a pot of coffee.

'So that's what I heard,' finished the page from the Poor Relation. He was closeted with Sir Philip in a small ante-room off the Hitchcocks's hall.

'Wait a bit,' said Sir Philip. 'Begin at the beginning, Tom, and let's have it again.'

The white-faced little page crinkled up his face in concentration. Although eleven years old, he already had that ancient knowing face of most London children. 'Big Jack, sir, is footman to Lady Stanton.'

'Yes, I remember her,' said Sir Philip. 'Nasty. Very nasty.'

'He starts bragging about how he's on a secret and dangerous mission,' said Tom. 'They all buy him drinks to see if they can loosen his tongue but he keeps dropping dark hints and patting the left-hand pocket of his coat as if to make sure something valuable is still there but never says nothing that makes sense.'

'Damme, boy, I wonder what it was.'

Tom grinned and thrust a hand into his short jacket pocket and brought out a blue glass bottle. 'This, mayhap,' he said. 'I picked his pocket.'

'Did you now? Stick by me, lad, and you'll go far.' Sir Philip held out his hand. 'Give it here.'

Tom handed it over. Sir Philip sniffed it and made a face. He had been familiar with that smell during his last bout of constipation. He stoppered the bottle up and said, 'Wait here.'

He darted off and studied the guest-list in the library. There was Lady Stanton's name. It was a long shot, but it could be that Lady Stanton meant to disgrace the poor relations by giving society a good dose of what was euphemistically referred to as the backyard trot. On the other hand, she could have sent her footman out to the apothecary and the silly footman could have considered his lady's bowels as a matter of great delicacy and secrecy.

He went back to the page. 'Just in case, Tom, I want you to wait until I change the contents of this bottle. I want you to take it back and leave it on the floor of the Running Footman hard by where this Jack was sitting.'

Sir Philip then went to the still room, poured the contents out of the blue bottle into an identical one, washed out Lady Stanton's bottle and filled it with plain water, and then returned and gave it to Tom, who sped off.

He almost collided in the doorway of the Running Footman with an agitated Jack who had just discovered that the precious bottle was missing. 'Looking for something?' asked Tom.

'I lost a little bottle here a while ago,' said Jack, walking into the tap and beginning to search around the area of floor where he had been sitting.

'Would this be it?' asked Tom, holding up the substitute bottle.

Jack seized it, his face crimson with relief. 'You are a good lad,' he said. 'Here's a penny for you.'

Tom took the penny. 'Best be off,' he said. 'At the Hitchcocks's getting ready for tonight. Lots to do.'

'I shall probably see you there,' said Jack, made chatty by relief. Normally he would have considered a page – and a hotel page at that – beneath him. 'I am escorting my lady but will visit the kitchens or the servants' hall.'

'My masters have high hopes of this evening,' said Tom. 'The food is fit for a king. Better, in fact. I doubt if His Majesty himself has tasted finer.'

'There's to be turtle soup?' asked Jack with an awful stagy casualness.

'Of course,' said Tom.

'I'm ever so partial to turtle soup myself,' said Jack. 'Might see if I can get a sip before it goes upstairs.'

'I'll wait for the leftovers as usual,' remarked Tom, his sharp little eyes scanning the footman's face.

'Wouldn't touch the soup afterwards,' said Jack earnestly.

'Why?'

'Cos turtle soup goes on the turn after a few hours . . . like cream.'

'Never heard o' that one.'

'Sure as sure. I've taken a liking to you, boy. Leave the soup alone.'

'And that's what he said,' reported Tom to Sir Philip half an hour later.

'So she's up to her old tricks,' mused Sir Philip. 'Well, well, we'll see what we can do.'

Mrs Budley and Miss Tonks found they had little time to get dressed that evening. Lady Fortescue and the colonel seemed to have been overcome by a sort of perfectionist desperation. Glasses which had been washed in soap and water and polished with a soft cloth were not considered shiny enough, and so she and Miss Tonks had been sent to the still room to prepare a glass polish by making a paste of calcined magnesia and purified benzine, and when that was ready, it was to be applied to every glass and they all had to be polished again.

Like Lady Macbeth trying to get the damned spot out, Mrs Budley scented her hands, but the smell of benzine seemed to cling to her skin. But at last she was ready and dressed in the new jaconet gown and with the silk flowers in her hair.

'You cannot possibly wear that!' screeched Miss Tonks.

Mrs Budley paused in the doorway. 'Why?'

Miss Tonks blushed delicately. 'You have fine shoulders, Eliza, but you are showing too much of them.'

Mrs Budley ran to the long glass. The low neckline exposed the top halves of her breasts. Yes, it *was* a trifle low but there was no time to change. The first guests would soon be arriving.

Lady Stanton had reverted to her more dashing style of dress with a view to catching the eye of the eligible marquess. It was an age when Fashion was based on the draping of Greek statuary: the minimum of clothes was still the fashion, causing one country girl to report on London ladies: 'They ran about with hardly any clothes on them and their faces painted red.' In fact, so red were the faces and so grand the feathered headdresses that often society women presented the appearance of some strange bejewelled aboriginal tribe. At the opera house, an experiment had been tried of posting doormen there for the express purpose of banning prostitutes, but the operation was cancelled after so many ladies of the *ton* had been refused entry.

Not that Lady Stanton seemed particularly naked, for she had covered every visible part of her body in thick white lead. Like a number of her peers, all expression on her face had to be shown in the eyes. One could not dare laugh or grimace for fear of causing cracks to run across the mask of white lead.

Lady Stanton was trusting to her footman to deal with the humiliation of the poor relations. She knew from past experience that to try to humiliate one of them in public would bring the malice of Sir Philip down on her head.

Although escorted to the ball by Mr Jasper Brackley, she planned to disengage herself from him as soon as she arrived. She wanted to advertise to the marquess that she was fancy-free.

Jack, the footman, was on the backstrap and had whispered that he had the bottle ready. It never crossed his simple mind that he might be doing something very wrong. Like Sir Philip, he had recognized the smell of senna pods and thought Lady Stanton merely meant to play a trick on society. He adored her. He thought that she was showing an endearingly puckish sense of humour.

No sooner had they arrived than Lady Stanton gave him a quick nod. His heart sang. Her escort, Mr Jasper Brackley, was looking at her curiously. It is *our* secret, thought Jack triumphantly.

He ran lightly down the area steps to the kitchens, which were in an uproar. How easy it was to fall into conversation with the kitchen servants. How miraculous that no one seemed to be looking his way when he lifted the great silver lid of the soup tureen and emptied the contents of that bottle into the turtle soup.

He had slain a dragon for his lady.

* * *

Mrs Budley was serving negus. Several of the matrons had been her friends in the past, but all affected not to know her. She had been prepared for this but it still made her long to throw the glasses of hot wine in their stupid faces.

In fact, she now regarded the whole of society with a jaundiced eye. A group of pinks of the *ton* were clustered around the champagne fountain, quaffing tankards of the stuff and laughing uproariously at a beefy-looking Corinthian who was holding forth.

His voice clearly reached Mrs Budley's ears.

'After giving a view holloa we ran off with the Charlies in full cry after us, when Sir George, who had purposely provided himself with a long cord, gave me one end and ran to the opposite end of Jermyn Street with the other in his hand holding it two feet above the pavement. The old Scouts came up in droves, and we had 'em down in a moment, for every mother's son of the guardians was caught in the trap, and rolled over each other, slap into the kennel. Never was such a prime bit of gig! One old buck got his jawbone broken; another staved in two of his crazy timbers, that is his ribs; a third bled from the nose like a pig; a fourth squinted admirably from a pair of painted peepers. Their number however increasing, we divided our forces and marched in opposite directions. Our party sallied along Bond Street, nailed up a nosy Charlie in his box and bolted with his lantern. The others weren't so fortunate, for the baronet's brother and his friends were safely lodged in St James's Watch House.'

98

This description of tormenting the watchmen, who were mostly elderly, was greeted with whoops of delight from the listeners. Then the laughter died and all the men round the fountain stared avidly towards the door. Lady Stanton came sailing in.

Mrs Budley's first thought was: How can I attract any man like Peterhouse with such women as this around?

Lady Stanton's muslin gown was so fine that it was like gauze and worn over a pink silk underdress and pink silk stockings, also so fine that they gave the naughty impression that she was wearing nothing underneath. Her heavy gold hair was ornamented with dyed ostrich feathers in rainbow colours. She had the height to carry such a headdress and she moved with a languid grace. She approached the fountain and then stood laughing as the men each rushed to fill a glass and hold it out to her.

'Lady Stanton,' muttered the colonel in her ear. Mrs Budley looked at her with renewed interest. This then was the lady who had been Harriet James's rival. She herself had never seen her before, as the trouncing of Lady Stanton had taken place in the hotel dining room, where Mrs Budley was rarely expected to be on duty.

And then, with a lurch of her heart, she saw the marquess standing in the doorway, magnificent in evening dress, accompanied by a tall friend.

Charles Manderley, for it was he, immediately joined the courtiers around Lady Stanton. The marquess walked forward to join him. Lady Stanton glowed at him, her feathered fan waving to and fro, the largeness of her eyes emphasized with kohl. Charles

Manderley said something and took her arm to lead her forward and introduce her.

And then the marquess saw Mrs Budley. He crossed to the table where she was serving negus, and to the amazement of the ladies gossiping about the table and holding glasses of the hot mixture, he made a low bow and said, 'Your servant, Mrs Budley.'

She swept a low curtsy. 'My lord. It is indeed a pleasure to see you again.'

'What are you doing here?' he asked, puzzled. 'Are you a friend of Mrs Hitchcock?'

'No, my lord. Mr and Mrs Hitchcock have engaged the services of the Poor Relation for this evening.'

'Do you need to do such a menial task yourself?' he asked, finding himself growing angry. He looked about him. 'There seem to be plenty of waiters and footmen.'

'Part of the deal is that we serve the guests ourselves. Do you wish a glass of negus, my lord?'

'No, I do not.' He looked curiously at the others. That must be Lady Fortescue, the one who was handing a glass of wine to a young buck with such hauteur that he was actually stammering out nervous thanks, and the tall old gentleman beside her was surely Colonel Sandhurst. Sir Philip he recognized despite that awful wig, and the thin, nervous female of indeterminate years with 'spinster' and 'poor relation' stamped all over her must be Miss Tonks.

He turned his attention back to Mrs Budley. She was a servant, and if he stood much longer talking to her, it would occasion comment. And yet, he was reluctant to leave. He had thought her a pretty and amiable lady, but now she looked alluring, with the well-cut gown showing those stunning breasts. In fact, the effect of those white mounds, partly revealed by the low neckline of the gown, combined with the open innocence in her eyes, was strangely seductive.

He found Charles Manderley with Lady Stanton beside him. Charles performed the introductions. The marquess bowed. 'Talking to the hired help, my lord?' asked Lady Stanton. 'You gentlemen of the *ton* are devils. Always ready to buss a pretty serving wench.'

'Mrs Budley is a friend,' said the marquess. He turned back to her. 'I have various requests from my tenants for your recipes, Mrs Budley. I shall talk to you later.'

He bowed and left, leaving Charles looking amused and speculative and Lady Stanton with narrowed eyes. She debated whether to have a glass of negus and then complain loudly about the quality of it but Mr Brackley appeared to remind her of their dance together and got a venomous look for his pains.

Only the thought that the marquess was in the ballroom and the fact that Sir Philip Sommerville was studying her closely made her shrug and acquiesce, although she called over her shoulder to Charles, 'Remember, the dance after this one is ours.'

The marquess dutifully danced with all the most eligible young ladies, mindful that he was supposed to be looking for a bride. He found he was dreading the moment when he would go in for supper with the other guests and have to watch Mrs Budley waiting table. He was still angry. There was no need for her to humiliate herself like this in front of society. He was so preoccupied in thinking about Mrs Budley that he hardly spared a thought for Lady Stanton, although she and Charles came over several times to speak to him between dances.

He decided to take Jessica Branston in to supper. He had met her before, he remembered, when her mother had claimed that carriage accident at his gates, and he was sorry for her, pitying her for having such a pushing mother.

Lady Stanton went in on the arm of Charles Manderley and Mr Brackley followed and promptly took the chair on her other side.

Sir Philip decided that Lady Stanton's fate would be decided on whether she drank the turtle soup or not. The poor relations flew between the long tables, serving food and pouring wine. The marquess noticed several of the men staring in a calculating way at Mrs Budley and making bold remarks. One even tried to get an arm around her waist, but as the angry marquess half-rose in his seat, Sir Philip went scurrying up and whispered something to the man, who flushed angrily and then sat and stared at his plate in a mortified way.

Mindful of his social duties, the marquess made small talk with Jessica while his mind raced over all the stories he had heard of hotel life. What indignities she must be subject to! Why, only the week before, Lord Byron had been drinking with his cronies at a hotel off Leicester Square. Men wishing to relieve themselves were supposed to use the backyard of the hotel but Lord Byron had used the front hall, on the carpet, and in full view of everybody . . .

'She didn't touch the soup,' hissed Sir Philip to Lady Fortescue.

'Who didn't?' asked Lady Fortescue, signalling to the waiters to take the soup plates away.

'Lady Stanton.'

'A pox on that whore,' remarked Lady Fortescue calmly. 'I do not care whether she drinks our soup or chokes on it.'

'You will see what you will see,' said Sir Philip mysteriously.

He scuttled down to the butler's pantry and part filled a decanter with wine fortified with brandy, guessing – rightly – that such as Lady Stanton would find unadulterated French wine too insipid. In fact, most wine dealers added brandy to their imported wines to suit the English taste. Then he poured the essence of senna pods into the decanter and carried it upstairs.

Lady Stanton was pretending to pay attention to what the gentlemen on either side of her were saying while all the time her eyes devoured the marquess, who was sitting almost opposite her at one of the long tables.

Sir Philip watched until her glass was empty and hurried up to refill it from the decanter. 'Our special vintage, my lady,' he whispered. 'There is a new fashion in France. It is quite *comme il faut* for the lady to ask the gentleman to take wine.'

There was a custom in the Regency of men asking ladies to 'drink with them'. This meant that the gentleman would raise his glass to a lady at the dinner or supper table and say, 'Will you take wine with me?'

and the lady was expected to match him glass for glass, or rather appear to, most ladies contenting themselves with sipping just a little.

So anxious was she to engage the marquess's attention that Lady Stanton never paused to reflect where the advice had come from. She raised her glass and said clearly, 'I take wine with you, Lord Peterhouse.' He looked mildly startled but politely raised his glass. Keeping her eyes fixed on him, Lady Stanton drank the contents of her glass. Mr Brackley sulkily refilled it, saying, 'You are making a cake of yourself. Ladies do not ask men to take wine with them.'

'They do in France,' snapped Lady Stanton in an angry aside. She raised her eyes again and, fixing the marquess with a burning look, again emptied her glass.

That was when disaster struck. Her lead paint cracked as wrenching pains seized her stomach and then the inevitable happened.

'Demme, smells like a sewer in here,' remarked Charles Manderley.

'I don't smell anything,' said Lady Stanton. 'Get me out of here,' she hissed to Mr Brackley.

'What?'

'You heard. Drape my shawl about my shoulders and walk closely behind me. Do it *now*.'

She rose to her feet. All the gentlemen round about her rose as well. Huddled in her long shawl, Lady Stanton almost ran from the room.

Sir Philip came up and removed the decanter. 'Goodness, this chair is stained,' he said loudly, looking down at where Lady Stanton had been sitting. He snapped his fingers and summoned a footman. 'Take this chair down to the kitchens and scrub it. Disgusting,' he said, shaking his head.

To the marquess, it seemed as if the supper would never end as course followed course and Mrs Budley flew here and there with plates and glasses. The food was superb. There were cries of delight when the guests were told to open the parcels at their places and all exclaimed over the gifts. When Despard, his eyes glittering with excitement, wheeled in the huge dessert, which was the whole of the Battle of Trafalgar executed in spun sugar down to the rigging on the ships, the guests burst into a spontaneous round of applause.

And then it was over. The band started up a jaunty tune in the ballroom and the guests began to file out, laughing and chattering.

'Now this is where the work really begins,' thought Mrs Budley, too tired now to even think about the marquess. The tables were rapidly cleared of dirty glasses and dishes. Lady Fortescue said to her, 'As soon as this is finished, we are to adjoin to a room on the first floor for our own supper. Very thoughtful of Mrs Hitchcock not to expect us to eat in the servants' hall.'

Gradually the room cleared of servants and then the poor relations made their way wearily upstairs to enjoy their own supper in peace and quiet.

Except Mrs Budley.

She sat down on a gilt chair in the supper room and put her head in her hands and let wave after wave of humiliation break over her head. She remembered the coarse remarks of some of the gentlemen and cursed herself on the folly of wearing too low-cut a gown. She saw the faces of guests she had known in her fashionable youth and remembered that all had cut her dead.

The music had changed. The sound of a waltz came from the ballroom, haunting and lilting.

'Mrs Budley?'

She looked up.

The marquess was standing there. He smiled down at her and held out his hand. 'Our dance, I think.'

'I cannot go in there, my lord!'

'We will dance here. Come.'

She looked at him in wonder as he raised her to her feet. He drew her into his arms and they waltzed, dipping and swaying, their steps matching. The tables were gone, apart from a long one against the wall which would shortly be restocked with bottles and glasses after the staff had enjoyed a brief respite. The champagne fountain had ceased to play and a group of bloated plaster cherubs which had only recently had rivers of champagne gushing from the horns they held in their plump hands gazed with sightless plaster eyes at the marquess and Mrs Budley as they circled round and round, as if enchanted.

Then the music ceased. She sank into a low curtsy. He bowed over her hand and then, as she rose, he jerked her into his arms and kissed her full on the mouth.

The hitherto sexually unawakened Mrs Budley came briefly to dazzling life. For one heady moment, her lips burnt under his own and her body strained against him.

Then a voice from the doorway said, 'Oh, I *do* beg your pardon,' with a very sarcastic intonation. The couple broke apart.

'My supper,' babbled Mrs Budley, and ran from the room.

The marquess stood alone and watched her go.

'Damn,' he said bitterly to the uncaring plaster cherubs. 'Damn and double damn!'

SIX

Kissing don't last; cookery do!

GEORGE MEREDITH

Usually after such a long and lavish affair as the Hitchcocks's ball, society members kept to their beds the following day, only venturing out to some mild entertainment in the evening. But now there was too much to gossip about, to talk about. The nabob's wife was now an established member of the *ton*. The glory of the food was praised in the West End and it was generally admitted that the bejewelled poor relations had been such *fun* and Sir Philip's waspish remarks were widely reported, for society loved to be insulted and Beau Brummell's popularity was proof of that.

But one group of ladies who met over the teacups at Lady Stanton's the following day, proved to be the exception to the general praise.

Mrs Tykes-Dunne said wearily it all had been too vulgar for worlds, Mrs Branston vowed that she would *faint* if Almack's lowered its high standards and let the Hitchcocks in through its august doors, and Lady Stanton remarked that the poor relations were obviously using inferior materials in the cooking, for she had never felt so ill in all her life.

Only Lady Fremley, stitching away with a little curved smile on her mouth, refrained from comment.

'Of course,' said Mrs Branston, rallying a little, 'I cannot help but be proud of my little Jessica. Did you mark how everyone stared when he took her in to supper? She is still quite in alt.'

Lady Fremley spoke for the first time. 'I am surprised you are here with us, Mrs Branston. Surely Lord Peterhouse will call in person today, as is the custom, to pay his respects to Jessica. I would have thought you would have preferred to wait at home.'

Mrs Branston's face darkened. 'He sent his servant,' she said curtly. Lady Stanton's mouth curved in her first smile of the day. Gentlemen only sent their servants in their place when the lady they had danced with the night before was considered too uninteresting to merit a personal call.

Lady Handon announced, 'Well, I have been saving a monstrous piece of news for all of you, regarding Peterhouse.'

They all looked at her. Even Lady Fremley stopped sewing.

'I thought I had left something in the supper room,' said Lady Handon. She had in fact noticed the marquess was not in the ballroom and had gone in search of him. 'The door to the supper room was closed, as the servants were supposed to be having their own supper. I opened it and guess what I saw!'

'What did you see?' asked Lady Stanton, casting an amused look around the rest.

'I saw the Marquess of Peterhouse kissing one of those poor relations, the little one with her dress half off.'

They gazed at her in dumb amazement. Lady Stanton was convulsed with fury. Her still weak stomach heralded another disaster, and with a muttered excuse she fled from the room.

The others stared at each other in consternation.

With the exception of Lady Fremley.

She picked up her sewing and said in a reflective voice, 'Well, that piece of news was certainly enough to make our hostess shite herself again.'

'*Really!*' cried Lady Handon and then sniggered. Mrs Branston began to giggle helplessly for the first time since she had been a schoolgirl, and Mrs Tykes-Dunne chortled happily.

Faintly from the privacy of a small room where the close-stool was lodged, Lady Stanton heard their laughter and her cheeks burnt with shame and her tortured body burnt with hate. Somehow, somewhere, and quite soon, she would be revenged on that pack of poor relations.

While the ladies were enjoying the humiliation of Lady Stanton, Bond Street was becoming crowded with afternoon strollers. It was not the most elegant of streets, but from two o'clock until five o'clock it was the resort of the most fashionable people. It became all bustle, all life, with the most elegant of carriages dashing up and down. The shops were full of trifles – confectionery, jewellery, cravats, books, perfumes, mezzotints, bric-à-brac; and there were coiffeurs, boot-makers and milliners.

Pierce Egan, the creator of the fictitious Corinthians, Tom and Jerry, described the magic of Bond Street: 'It makes the lord who drives four-in-hand forget his losses of the night before at some of the fashionable gaming houses. It makes one adventurer forget that the clothes in which he expects to gain respect and attention are more than likely to be paid for in Newgate; another for a time forgets that John Doe and Richard Doe have expelled him from his lodgings; and a third that all his worldly possessions are not equal to the purchase of a dinner. It is an *ignis fatuus* – a sort of magic lantern replete with delusive appearances – of momentary duration – an escape to the regions of noise, tumult, vanity and frivolity, where the realities of life, the circumstances and the situation of the observer, are not suffered to intrude . . .'

It was this heady atmosphere of the-devil-take-tomorrow which usually buoyed up the spirits of the poor relations, and even Miss Tonks during these hectic afternoons felt like a wicked adventuress, a woman of mystery, a woman with hidden charms which some gentleman one day would surely discover. Living in Bond Street meant living in an unreal world and never was that world more unreal than during the Season, when families would bankrupt their estates in the country in order to appear elegant in London. But the Poor Relation benefited from the more solid aristocratic families, the more prudent ones, who knew that lodging at the Poor Relation gave them social cachet without the dreadful expense of renting a whole house and engaging an army of servants for the Season. The food at the Poor Relation was so famous that residents could entertain guests in the dining room and gain as much social credit as if they had thrown an expensive ball.

Mrs Budley, who believed she had been *aged* by love, often felt she was the only one of them who realized the precariousness of an existence based on fickle fashion. Only she, she felt, knew that their future actually lay in the hands of Despard, the French cook. Sir Philip had told them in confidence that Despard was actually an escaped prisoner from the hulks and therefore was forced to stay loyal to them for his own safety.

But Mrs Budley did not trust the cook, who sneered at the aristocracy as effete, and she often thought that when he had squirrelled away enough money, he would desert them and try to make his way back to his home country. Certainly, for the moment, he appeared drunk with success and confident that the Poor Relation would receive more orders for outside catering.

Mrs Budley went about her work, trying to forget about that kiss. She had not confided in Miss Tonks, although she longed to speak to someone. A concerned Miss Tonks might tell the others. But who would tell her other than that she had no hope of marriage?

The drama of the fire in the hotel had brought Harriet and her duke together. But there seemed to be no dramas ahead in her life. Only hard work.

She did, however, feel a certain feminine lightness of heart when they all met in the sitting room as usual that evening and Lady Fortescue announced that as the Hitchcocks had been so generous and as Lord Ager in Berkeley Square had sent round a request that they do the catering for his daughter's coming-out ball, she was prepared to loosen the purse-strings and allow them all to buy something each. As Lord Ager's ball was to be in a month's time, the ladies could have the luxury of having gowns made for them by a couturier. Sir Philip leaned forward, his eyes shining with greed. What should he buy? If the ladies were to have expensive gowns, then there would surely be no objection of him ordering a coat from Weston, the famous tailor. One is never old in one's mind's eye. Sir Philip saw himself in a blue coat of Bath superfine, slim and elegant as he had been in his youth.

One of the strollers that day in Bond Street was Mr George Pym, nephew of the late marquess and cousin to the present one. He had lived in hope for years that the present marquess would be killed in battle, leaving him free to inherit the title. As if conjured up by his thoughts, he saw the marquess standing outside the Poor Relation Hotel, looking up at it. He saw him make a half-move to go inside and then walk on. Mr Pym hurried to catch up with him.

'Good day, Rupert,' he called. The marquess turned round and looked down at Mr Pym, thinking not for the first time that he was an unlikeable man. Mr Pym was small and round and owlish, the birdlike appearance being emphasized by the cut-away front of his coat and the long tails at the back.

'Doing the Season, George?' asked the marquess.

'Tol rol. One must,' said Mr Pym. 'Got miserable lodgings, however.'

The marquess knew Mr Pym to be very rich indeed but obviously still as mean as ever. He had no intention of offering him house-room, so he ignored the remark.

'And why are you here?' pursued Mr Pym. 'Did not think jauntering about was much in your line.'

'Oh, but I am in Town to find a bride.'

Mr Pym glared up at him. A married marquess meant a quiverful of little heirs to stand between him and the title. Certainly the marquess looked very fit, but London was full of plagues and humours – cholera, typhoid, smallpox, influenza, diptheria – any of those beautiful maladies guaranteed to take one strong marquess to his early grave.

Charles Manderley approached them and the marquess hailed him with relief. 'Excuse us, George,' he said. He linked arms with Charles and they strolled off.

Mr Pym went into Limmer's to comfort his soul with gin punch. He recognized practically everyone in the room, most society members knowing each other, if only by sight. He saw Mr Jason Brackley and went to join him.

'Didn't see you at the Hitchcocks's,' remarked Mr Brackley by way of greeting.

'Was invited,' said Mr Pym, 'but folks were saying it was an unfashionable affair.'

'Wasn't,' said Mr Brackley, equally elliptic. 'Well done. Food a poem. Had to leave early. I squired Lady Stanton and she became ill. Heard some gossip about that cousin of yours, though.'

'Who? Peterhouse?'

'The same.'

'What's he been up to?'

'Caught kissing a serving wench.'

'So? We've all done that.'

'No ordinary serving wench. One of the owners of the Poor Relation Hotel.'

'Same thing. She's in trade, ain't she?'

'Don't know about that. Tell you a story. My fickle love was enamoured of the Duke of Rowcester.'

'Who is your fickle love?'

'Lady Stanton.'

Mr Pym gave a mock sigh. 'Rapture. A divine lady.'

'Exactly. But she lost Rowcester, if you but recall. He married that hotel cook, Harriet James.'

'Oh, I remember *that*,' said Mr Pym. 'But everyone knew Harriet James. Good family.'

'Quite. Well, the lady he was kissing was Mrs Eliza Budley, widow of Jack, formerly Eliza Tremaine, and the Tremaines are as aristocratic as you or I.'

Mr Pym's face darkened. 'Don't want anyone like *her* in the family,' he sneered.

Mr Brackley's eyes crinkled up with malice.

'If you take my advice, dear fellow, you'll start getting used to the idea.'

Jack, the second footman, stood before his mistress with his head bowed.

'So,' she said coldly, 'you allowed yourself to be gulled like the veriest flat. The hotel page must have taken that bottle from you and replaced it with one with harmless contents. I have no room in my household for useless servants.'

Jack sank to one knee. 'Pray order me to do anything, my lady. But do not send me away.'

She turned away from him and strode up and down the room. 'I must have revenge.'

'I-I h-heard something, my l-lady, which might be useful,' stammered Jack.

She stopped and glared down at her still kneeling footman. 'Out with it!'

'If you please, my lady, I heard that Lord Ager has employed the hotel to do the catering for his daughter's come-out.'

'So?'

'At the Hitchcocks's, he sent a note down to the kitchen to the hotel cook, Despard, a Frenchman, offering him a fortune to join his household. Despard refused. I was there in the kitchen at the time. One of the scullions muttered something about Despard being an escaped French convict from the hulks and he could not leave the hotel or Sir Philip would betray him.'

She stood studying the footman and then a slow smile curved her lips. 'Get to your feet. I still have a use for you.'

He rose and looked at her with hope in his eyes.

'Take away that cook of theirs,' she said half to herself, 'and you take away most of their cachet. So he is bound to Sir Philip. You must sound him out, find if he wishes to escape back to France, and if he does, we will pay him handsomely to run away. Can you do that?'

116

'Oh, yes, my lady.'

'Then set to it!'

The following day was fine and sunny. The full quota of maids and waiters and footmen was on duty, and so Lady Fortescue suggested that Mrs Budley should go out for a walk and get some fresh air. Normally Mrs Budley would have asked Miss Tonks to go with her and they would certainly have taken one of the footmen with them, but a longing to be on her own and think about the marquess kept her silent. It showed the change that had taken place in Mrs Budley that she should even contemplate facing the streets of London. Certainly, when the poor relations had first found her, she had been alone in Hyde Park but in such a state of misery that she had not noticed the broad comments, the leers and winks from passing bucks. But now that she had been used to a certain amount of protection, it was unusual that she should decide to forgo it.

She had entered her marriage with the firm belief that men were the stronger sex and knew better about everything and anything, a very common view in an age when the streets were so violent that men had to know how to protect themselves, when practically all the money-earning jobs were given to men. Even the corset-makers were men. Women were expected to be pretty, silly dolls, and before, Mrs Budley had not questioned that view. But she had had much to endure over her longings for the marquess and she felt she was coping with it quite well. Also, daily contact with Sir

Philip Sommerville was enough to make the weakest and most feminine lady learn to stand up for herself.

So she carefully dressed in a very plain drab walking dress and a hat with a veil and escaped out into Bond Street, feeling the warm sun strike through her veil, feeling spring in the air, drinking in that heady devil-may-care feeling emanating from the shifting, busy, fashionable crowd.

The marquess saw her. Despite the veil and the plain dress, he recognized her and quickened his step until he caught up with her.

'Mrs Budley!'

She stopped, her heart racing, and looked up at him, realizing in that instant that this was just what she had been hoping for, not time to be by herself and think, but to be alone in the hope that he would come across her. She put back her veil, vaguely proud of the fact that her hands did not tremble.

'Where are you going? May I escort you? You should not be out unescorted.'

'I am not going anywhere in particular,' she said. 'Lady Fortescue suggested I get some fresh air.'

'Then let us be very unfashionable and walk to the Green Park. I wish to talk to you.'

He took her arm and they walked along. She wished she had lowered her veil as he nodded and said 'Good day' to various people.

He talked easily of the ball and what a success it had been. Mrs Budley replied by saying that his neighbour, Lord Ager, had engaged their services for his daughter's ball and the marquess remarked with an edge in his voice that he could not understand her equanimity at a further prospect of appearing in the public eye as a servant, to which Mrs Budley said sadly, 'Ah, but you have never been poor.'

When they reached the park behind its high brick walls and were walking along by the reservoir, he remembered Mrs Appleton's request and asked her for the recipes. 'I will write them out and send you copies,' she said, to which he replied, 'Thank you,' and she immediately felt depressed because he had not offered to call and see her and collect them in person.

They both came to a stop and stared down into the waters of the reservoir, their reflections blurred and distorted by a flurry of breeze. 'I am glad of this opportunity to talk to you, Mrs Budley,' he said. 'I must apologize for my behaviour at the ball.'

How she had dreamt of that kiss, memorized the feel of it, how he had looked! And he was apologizing for the most enchanting thing that had happened to her in the whole of her life. She felt a lump rising in her throat but she said gamely if stiffly, 'Your apology is accepted.'

'It will not happen again,' he said, adding insult to injury. 'I feel I took advantage of your position.'

She had once gone with the others to see the illuminations at the Spanish Embassy and they had stayed and watched the spectacle and then had watched the lamps being extinguished one by one until the whole building was in blackness. That was what this felt like: all her little lamps of hope and romance were being snuffed out one by one as the full import of his words sank into her. He had kissed her as he would a pretty serving wench in a tavern. She looked around in a bewildered way, as if wondering why the day was still so normal and sunny. A dowager made her stately way past like a galleon, with her footman walking a pace behind carrying her pug-dog. A child ran with an iron hoop. Two guardsmen talked loudly of the money they had lost the night before.

She raised her hands and lowered her veil. How bravely and determinedly she had left him after Gunter's, saying she would not see him again. Why had she ventured out on this stupid walk? If Letitia had been with her, they would have exchanged a few pleasantries with him and gone on their way.

She shivered a little despite the warmth of the day. 'I must return,' she said. 'I have my duties to attend to.'

He held out his arm but she suddenly could not face walking back with him, enduring those curious stares. Better to get away from him as soon as possible.

'Please do not trouble,' she said. 'I am late.' She picked up her skirts and ran away from him towards the lodge on Piccadilly. He made a half-step to follow her and then decided against it.

But he felt quite lost and hurt, almost as if she had slapped his face.

Jack, the second footman, waited impatiently for Sunday to arrive, guessing that was the only day when Despard would have any free time. He himself had been given all the free time from his duties that he wanted in order to secure the disappearance of the French chef, and he had spent most of it out of livery, hanging about Bond Street, watching the comings and goings from the area of the hotel, hoping to see the cook perhaps come up to take the air.

By Sunday morning, he was feeling desperate and heaved a sigh of relief when he recognized Despard's white and twisted face under a broad-brimmed black hat surfacing from the basement.

He fell into step behind him, determined to see where he went and start up a conversation with him. The cook walked as far as Soho Square and turned in at the door of the Catholic church. Jack hovered helplessly outside. His family were Nonconformists and he felt if he stepped inside a Catholic church, the devil would get his soul. He waited for a long time, beginning to wonder whether the church had a back entrance or not. To his infinite relief, he at last saw the figure of the cook emerge. He fell into step behind him again, hoping he would not return to the hotel but go first to some chop-house where there would be a better chance of starting a conversation.

But when the chef began to head straight for Bond Street, Jack plucked up his courage. He dare not return to his mistress again with any tale of failure. He quickened his step and said tentatively, 'Monsoor Despard?'

The cook did not slacken his pace. On the contrary, he walked faster than ever.

'Monsoor!' called Jack desperately. 'I am a friend. I can get you money. I can get you back to France.'

Despard stopped. He turned slowly round and looked the tall footman up and down.

'Speak,' he commanded.

'Not here,' said Jack urgently. 'Let us find a quiet coffee house or tavern.'

'On a *Sunday*?'

'The Running Footman,' said Jack eagerly. 'We knock at the back door on a Sunday.'

'Very well. But make it quick.'

Jack led the way and soon they were being let in through the back door of the Running Footman and into the shadowy tap where other servants were cheerfully breaking the laws of the Sabbath. Jack called for a bottle of the best burgundy, mindful of the generous expenses he was being allowed. Despard eyed the footman narrowly. He recognized him now. This was Lady Stanton's servant, he who had tried to doctor the turtle soup. Sir Philip had said that if he was spotted slipping anything into the tureen, to look the other way.

'What are you plotting now?' asked Despard, whose English had improved in leaps and bounds since Sir Philip had rescued him from the dock of the Old Bailey, his accent a mixture of French and Cockney.

'What do you mean, "plotting"? I am here to help you.'

'You put something in the soup at the Hitchcocks's, but Sir Philip was wise to your game. What now? Don't pretend you mean to help me in any way, mon brave. That mistress of yours wants revenge.'

Jack looked at him gloomily. He had not expected Despard to be wise to his mistress's schemes. Complete honesty now was the only hope.

He shrugged in what he hoped was a worldly way. 'No use trying to pull the wool over your eyes. All right. Here's the score. Lady Stanton knows that the reputation of the hotel is now based on your cooking and not on the fact that a bunch of genteel paupers have turned to trade. To that end, she wants you out of the hotel and on your road to France before Lord Ager's ball. She's prepared to pay you enough to set you up for life in a restaurant of your own.'

'Very fine,' sneered Despard. 'All she has to do is give me the money, I get false papers, she reports me to the authorities and she gets what she wants, her money back, and me in prison, as well as Sir Philip and the others being disgraced.'

Adoration for his mistress had quickened Jack's normally slow brains. 'I could get her to sign something,' he said, 'which implicates her, which would be your guarantee of safety.'

'You are serious about this,' Despard said. He sipped his wine and half closed his eyes. He could *smell* France, where the sun seemed to shine more than it did in this grey and foggy country. He would be free of the hated English. He would be his own man. 'How much?' he asked finally.

Jack named a sum which made Despard's eyes blink rapidly. With money like that he would have no more worries. He could start his own restaurant. Through the network of French immigrants, some not loyal to the English, he knew where he could get false papers – at a price.

'The money would need to be in gold,' he said.

'Gold it is,' said Jack. 'Come with me now to my mistress. You will feel better after you have discussed it with her.'

'Very well,' said Despard. 'But make it quick.'

Jack presented Despard to his mistress with all the flourish of a knight laying a dragon at his lady's feet.

Despard eyed Lady Stanton narrowly and began: 'I should explain the terms I wish, in case your servant here has been too hasty. The money must be in gold.'

'Agreed,' said Lady Stanton.

'And in order to protect myself, as I shall be travelling under false papers, I wish you to sign a document explaining your part in this affair – otherwise you could have me arrested.'

Lady Stanton glared at Jack. 'You agreed to this?'

'It seemed the only way,' said Jack.

'I do not wish to be implicated,' she said flatly.

Despard turned to go.

'No! Wait!' she cried. 'Cannot you take my word I will not betray you?'

He turned back. 'Milady, I am an artist, and you, in order to get revenge, were prepared to make all the guests at that ball ill. Oh, yes, Sir Philip told me your plan. No, I do not trust you. Not without that piece of paper.'

She bit her lip. 'Oh, very well,' she snapped. 'But I wish you to leave as soon as possible. How long will it take you to get these papers?'

'Provided you let me have the gold, four or five days.'

124

'Come here after midnight tomorrow and I will have the money for you. But you will have no letter from me until you are actually on the Dover stage.'

He nodded curtly and left.

Lady Stanton rounded on her footman. 'I should not have sent a country bumpkin like you to arrange such a delicate matter. Someone with more wit and sophistication would never have agreed to my signing any paper. You may go.'

Smarting with humiliation, Jack slouched out. Love had changed to hate. Somehow, somewhere, he would turn this affair to his advantage.

The next night, Mrs Budley tossed and turned in bed. In her mind she walked once more in the Green Park with the marquess. Why had she felt so hurt? His apology had been that of a gentleman. Why had she not flirted instead of running away? Worry and sleeplessness were making her hungry, for she had eaten little that day. She sighed and rose and dressed. She would go next door to the hotel kitchen and find something to eat.

She picked up the spare key she kept which fitted the servants' door at the foot of the area steps, and made her way next door. Bond Street was still full of bustle, with fashionables moving from one party to the other. She slipped down the area steps, opened the door and walked through to the kitchen, where the banked-up fire burnt with a dull red glow in the kitchen range. She lit a candle. The clock in the corner chimed one in the morning, one single silvery note. She swung the kettle over the fire. And then she heard the sound of someone coming down the area steps. Despard! And the French cook loathed anyone in his kitchen when he was not there!

She swung the kettle back, blew out the candle, and moved towards the door which led to the back stairs leading up to the hall. Something made her pause outside the door, leave it open a crack, and look through.

Despard, a shadowy shape at first, until he lit the candle by thrusting it through the bars of the grate, moved about the kitchen. He was clutching a heavy wash-leather bag which he finally put down on the table. Then he sat down and looked at it steadily, his odd face elated.

Mrs Budley went quietly up the stairs. She blinked in the sudden flood of light in the hall from the great chandelier.

'Why up so late?' demanded Sir Philip, appearing out of the office.

'I couldn't sleep,' said Mrs Budley. 'I went down to the kitchen to get something to eat, but I heard Despard coming back and so I ran away. You know what he is like. He hates any of us being in his kitchen. Something made me pause and stand by the door and look in. He placed a heavy wash-leather bag on the table, the kind used to carry money, and he gazed at it and there was a look of elation and triumph on his face. People are getting used to us now. Despard's cooking is the attraction. He does not like us English and I always fear he will escape.'

'He can't very well do that,' said Sir Philip, 'but I would like to know what is in that bag. Go into the office and wait there. I was having a bite to eat myself and there is some wine and cold pie on the desk.'

One thing about Sir Philip, thought Mrs Budley, was that despite his waspishness, he was always ready to cope with whatever came up. Because of his reputation, the staff were saved from the usual humiliating behaviour meted out to the staff at other hotels.

Sir Philip went down to the kitchen. Despard was sitting at the kitchen table, drinking wine.

'You were out tonight,' said Sir Philip. 'Where did you go?'

'Where I go in my free time is my business,' said the cook.

'I wonder. Remember, if I find you are thinking of running away from us, I will turn you over to the authorities. I would never have got you out of the Old Bailey had I told them that you were actually an escaped French prisoner from the hulks. What is in that bag?'

'My business.'

Sir Philip seized the bag and opened the string and shook it upside down. A large hare fell out on the table. 'Friend gave it to me,' said Despard laconically.

Sir Philip felt rather silly. Despard was the same old Despard.

He nodded and went out. Despard grinned. He had heard the light patter of feet on the steps as Mrs Budley had made her retreat and had hidden the gold from the bag and popped the dead hare into it.

'Nothing in that bag but a dead hare,' said Sir Philip, walking into the office. 'It's lack of sleep. It's giving you fancies.'

'Possibly,' said Mrs Budley reluctantly. And yet, would Despard have sat there looking at a bag containing a dead hare with such elation? And it had been an expensive wash-leather bag, not the kind of article a cook would sully with dead game.

'My duties in the hotel are light at present,' she went on. 'I have always longed to be able to cook well. I must think of my future. Should anything happen to you or Lady Fortescue or the colonel, it would be pleasant to think I was qualified to earn my living doing something. I think I shall ask Despard to train me in his art.'

'Despard allow you near his precious cooking pots? Think again.'

But the very next day, Mrs Budley approached Despard with her request. He looked at her sourly. 'I have no time to train amateurs,' he snapped, 'especially women.'

'I write a fair hand,' wheedled Mrs Budley. 'Would you not like to publish your recipes one day? Cannot you see your name on the title page?'

Despard paused stirring sauce and eyed her speculatively. He thought he would like to leave some record of his success in England. Besides, with him gone, they would need to find a new cook. He owed them all something for his freedom. The new cook would be helped if his recipes were written down.

'Very well,' he said.

Mrs Budley opened a dimity bag she had brought with her and took out a cap and apron.

'I'll begin now.'

SEVEN

Thou art a traitor:
Off with his head!

WILLIAM SHAKESPEARE

Mrs Budley's suspicions grew in the next few days as she worked busily in the kitchen. There was an air of suppressed excitement emanating from Despard, and occasionally he slipped out, and peering up through the window, she could see that he was talking to someone in the street outside, although all she saw of that someone was a pair of stocky legs ending in square-toed buckled shoes. But she kept her suspicions to herself, something she was shortly to regret.

She *had* been going to have another talk with Sir Philip about the cook, but something happened which drove it out of her mind. She had sent the recipes to the marquess and that had given her an almost comfortable feeling of finality, a feeling that had enabled her to concentrate on cooking in the sweaty heat of the kitchen and forget about her appearance. She was bending over a sauce-pot, conscious of Despard's jealous eyes on her, when Miss Tonks appeared in the kitchen, looking flustered.

'Lord Peterhouse is called,' she said. 'He wishes to see you. I explained it was not very convenient but he only smiled and said he would wait.'

'Oh,' said Mrs Budley stupidly. Despard took the wooden spoon from her and edged in front of her. Mrs Budley looked wildly down at her old gown and then raised her hands to her tousled fluffy hair under the white skull-cap.

'Go up the area steps and run next door and change,' urged Miss Tonks.

'Where is he?'

'In the office.'

Mrs Budley shook her head. 'He knows I work here. There is no need to change.' And with Miss Tonks exclaiming and twittering in distress, she made her way up the back stairs to the hall. By appearing in front of him in her work clothes, she wanted to kill all her hopes, all her nonsensical hopes of romance.

'Leave me, Letitia,' she said, and walked into the office.

The marquess, who had been sitting behind the desk, rose at her entrance. Immediately she saw him, she wished with all her heart she had followed Letitia's advice and changed. The marquess looked very tall, very grand, very remote. His coat of blue superfine would have made Sir Philip swoon with envy, his cravat was a sculptured work of starch and muslin, his leather breeches moulded his strong thighs like a second skin, and his top-boots shone like black glass. He swept off his hat and bowed.

His hooded, veiled eyes showed nothing of what he

was thinking, which was just as well for Mrs Budley. The marquess was angry with her, angry that she should dare to present herself to him in a shabby dress, apron, messy hair and servant's skull-cap.

But he said politely enough, 'I came in person to thank you for the recipes.'

'You are most welcome, my lord.'

His odd eyes suddenly flashed with temper. 'Do you have to look like a scullion?'

She put her hands up to her suddenly hot cheeks. 'I work here,' she said defiantly.

'I was received by Lady Fortescue, who was wearing a very fine morning gown. Miss Tonks, in lilac silk, was sent to fetch you. I heard Lady Fortescue remark to Colonel Sandhurst that Sir Philip had gone to Weston's to see how his new coat was coming along. Are you determined to martyr yourself?'

'You do not understand,' she cried. 'Our reputation now largely lies in the hands of our French cook. Were he to quit, we could lose everything.'

'This hotel,' he said contemptuously, 'obsesses you all. I have friends who turn their lives and their every waking thought over to their country homes. That is more understandable since such homes have been part of their families for centuries. But this shoddy place, which depends on the whims of society, is another thing.'

All her life, Mrs Budley had meekly thought that men knew better and had bowed her head before their judgements. But now her eyes sparkled and she said defiantly, 'I am *proud* to be a part of this concern. How could such as you understand? What do you know of the indignities of being a poor relation? What do you know of being despised and pitied and humiliated?'

The others would not have recognized their dainty and feminine Mrs Budley in the lady with heightened colour and flashing eyes. In a milder tone of voice, she went on. 'I am sure you have much to do, my lord, and as you can see, I am very busy.' She opened the door of the office and walked out into the hall.

Mr George Pym, who had been about to enter the hotel, shrank back into the shadow of the entrance and watched avidly.

The marquess looked down at Mrs Budley and his anger melted. He no longer saw the shabby gown or noticed her fly-away hair. He saw her glowing skin and large eyes and the swell of her bosom under her apron.

He raised her hand to his lips. 'I shall call on you again,' he said, 'if I may.'

'As you will, my lord,' said Mrs Budley weakly, feeling the pressure of those lips against her hand.

Mr Pym walked away without entering the hotel. Something must be done about this. He could hardly put a spoke in the marquess's wheel if the man were courting a respectable miss at her first Season. But surely it should be easy to nip such a budding relationship.

Charles Manderley was the best bet, he thought suddenly. For all his easy manners, the man was a high stickler.

Mr Pym tried the coffee houses and clubs, finally running his quarry to earth in the middle of St James's.

'Got something very important to tell you,' said Mr Pym. 'It concerns Rupert.'

Charles looked at him haughtily. He was not in the best of moods. He had expected to bed Lady Stanton and she had proved elusive. When he did see her, she was always chaperoned by some elderly Scottish female and her conversation, if that is what it could be called, consisted of plying him with questions about his friend Peterhouse.

'If you consider yourself a friend of his,' continued Mr Pym, 'you'll listen to what I have to say.'

'Step into White's with me,' said Mr Manderley impatiently. 'I hope you are not wasting my time.'

He entered the club, nodding a greeting to the dandies in the bay window before leading the way to a table in the corner of the coffee room.

'Out with it,' he said.

'Rupert is courting a servant,' said Mr Pym.

'My friend's affairs are no concern of mine.'

'I think Rupert may have marriage in mind.'

Charles looked amused. 'We do not marry servants,' he said, speaking for the whole of the ruling class.

'This is no ordinary servant. She is Mrs Budley, widow of Jack, one of the Tremaines. She is part-owner of the Poor Relation.'

'Then she has put herself beyond marriage. Rupert is setting up a flirt.'

'He was seen kissing her passionately at the Hitch-cocks's ball and only today I saw him taking leave of her at the hotel. She was dressed like a kitchen girl in cap and apron and yet he bowed before her and kissed her hand. The man is in love. You must stop him from making a fool of himself.'

'Sounds like a hum to me,' said Charles with an easiness he did not feel. 'I'll speak to Rupert, but, mark you, he'll laugh in my face!'

Charles Manderley was unable to find the marquess that day and he found himself later in Lady Stanton's drawing room. As usual, she led the conversation round to the marquess and Charles snapped, 'Peterhouse is romancing Mrs Budley, one of the owners of the Poor Relation.'

Lady Stanton kept an expression of polite interest on her face as she said blandly, 'My friends were making a great fuss because Peterhouse was caught kissing this creature at the Hitchcocks's ball, but whenever did us ladies trouble our heads over kisses given to a servant?'

'No ordinary servant,' he said darkly. 'I've been trying to find Peterhouse to put him wise. He cannot disgrace his family name.'

'Exactly,' agreed Lady Stanton. 'A brief affair would be one thing, but marriage with such as she is out of the question. I pity the poor thing, for I should not like to be in such a predicament myself.'

And Charles, who thought that marriage with such as Lady Stanton was out of the question and saw his hopes of an affair finally dashed, left for the opera later that evening in a thoroughly bad temper.

He was fortunate in finding the marquess. He joined him in his box. The marquess was entertaining a certain Sir Roger Arnold, his wife and his very pretty daughter. Something of his temper eased as Charles looked into the fair if foolish features of Belinda Arnold. In his eyes, she was just the sort of lady his friend should marry. He settled down to enjoy the company and put all thoughts of interfering in his friend's life out of his head. That was until the opera ball. Having found no lady himself to spark his fancy, he could not help noticing that the marquess was looking increasingly bored with the fair Belinda and several times did not even seem to hear what she said to him.

So after the Arnolds had been escorted home, he suggested to the marquess that they go to Wader's at the corner of Bolton Street and play a rubber of whist.

'Stakes are crazily high there,' said the marquess. 'But I'll share a bottle of wine with you to end the evening.'

After they had drunk almost the whole bottle and had chatted easily on various topics, Charles said casually, 'What is all this I am hearing about you romancing a certain Mrs Budley?'

The marquess's black eyes frosted over. In cold, chilly, autocratic accents, he said, 'I do not discuss Mrs Budley with you or anyone else, Charles. Now, shall we broach another bottle, or do you wish to play? Do not expect me to join you at the tables, however. I am become prudent in my old age.'

Charles now felt thoroughly alarmed. The marquess had blocked any mention of Mrs Budley in the haughty way a gentleman refused to discuss any lady whom he regarded highly.

He talked away easily, he said he might play after all, and the marquess took his leave. Charles Manderley made up his mind. He would need to speak to Mrs Budley and warn that little adventuress off. Like most Lotharios, he did not have much respect or indeed liking for women. The fact that the couple might be falling in love did not cross his mind. The sexes fell into two categories, hunter and hunted. Rupert in this case was the hunted and it had to stop.

It was the hotel page who told Mrs Budley the next day that there was a gentleman to see her. This time, she decided, she would be properly dressed. Confident that her caller was the marquess and elated that he should want to see her again so soon, she told the page to put him in the office and serve him with wine and then ran next door to the room she shared with Miss Tonks and scrambled into a pretty muslin gown and pelisse, and brushed and dressed her hair.

Despard thought the gods were taking care of him as he watched her go. He rapped out orders to the kitchen staff as to what had to be done, said he was stepping out for a few moments, put on his coat and hat and picked up a stout corded trunk, which he had placed beside the area door that morning, and made his escape. The Dover coach did not leave for another two hours, plenty of time to get to the City and make sure that Lady Stanton had sent the letter he needed to the coaching inn.

Charles Manderley looked up in surprise at Mrs Budley when she entered the office. His first thought was that she was much younger than he had expected. He had seen her at the ball when she had been serving negus, but had not paid very much attention to her. But he could see from the disappointment in her large eyes, quickly veiled, that she had been expecting the marquess.

'I am come,' he began, after introducing himself, 'as a friend of Peterhouse.'

How those eyes of hers suddenly lit up!

'There is a silly rumour going around that Peterhouse is enamoured of you.' He gave a light laugh. 'Ridiculous, is it not? But I am anxious to see my friend settled in marriage, and such rumours, should they reach the ears of his intended, might do damage.'

Her hand fluttered towards her bosom and then dropped. 'Intended?' she echoed.

'Yes, a Miss Belinda Arnold, one of our fairest beauties, all that is suitable. Have pity on Peterhouse, Mrs Budley. You have chosen to ruin your reputation; do not ruin his chances of a happy marriage by continuing to pursue him.'

'Believe me, Mr Manderley, I have no intention of doing so,' said Mrs Budley haughtily, 'and I have not been pursuing him.'

The office door opened and Sir Philip walked in. He had sensed trouble.

'Mrs Budley,' said Sir Philip, 'you must not entertain gentlemen in this office with the door closed.'

'Mrs Budley is safe with me,' snapped Charles.

'You're Manderley, ain't you?' said Sir Philip, who remembered him from his first meeting with the marquess. 'London's latest whore-monger.'

'How dare you!' shouted Charles. 'Were you not so antique, I would call you out.'

'Were I not so antique, I would throw you out,' countered Sir Philip. 'The ladies of this hotel are my concern. What is your business here with Mrs Budley?'

'He has come to tell me I am ruining the Marquess of Peterhouse's hopes. The marquess wishes to marry a certain Miss Arnold.'

'And what has our Mrs Budley got to do with Peterhouse's hopes or chances?' asked Sir Philip.

'Simply that Mrs Budley's behaviour has occasioned comment,' said Charles stiffly, wishing he had not come.

'See here,' said Sir Philip, 'Mrs Budley's behaviour is and always was beyond reproach. Take yourself off, you young pup, and don't come sniffing round here again.'

'Gladly,' said Charles, and gathering up what Sir Philip had left of his dignity, he marched out.

Mrs Budley sat down on a high-backed chair and stared bleakly in front of her.

'What's all this then?' wheedled Sir Philip. 'What have you been up to? We all know you got a little bit taken with his lordship when you were in Warwickshire, but we felt sure that was all over. I had hopes for you myself. I even engineered that fire so you could get to talk to him again. But nothing came of it . . . did it?'

'He kissed me at the Hitchcocks's ball,' said Mrs Budley, too miserable to cry.

'Gentlemen will kiss willing ladies. I thought you knew that you were in a position at that ball that might leave you open to insult were you not careful. That gown you had on, for a start . . .'

'I know, I know,' she said wretchedly. 'He called here yesterday to thank me for some recipes. He kissed my hand and said he would call again.'

Sir Philip studied her. It could be that the marquess was interested in her. With Mrs Budley out of the way, that would leave four. If only he could get rid of Miss Tonks and Colonel Sandhurst, that would leave him blissfully alone with Lady Fortescue. Still, Mrs Budley would be a start.

'If he is courting someone, he had no right to look at me so . . . and . . . and . . .' Mrs Budley looked at Sir Philip helplessly.

Sir Philip patted her hand. 'It'll happen if it's meant to happen. Say your prayers and keep out of that kitchen or you'll have red hands and smell of grease. No need for it.'

'As to that, I cannot shake off a suspicion that Despard means to cut and run.'

'Take it from me, Despard won't dare. Leave the cooking pots alone.'

Again, despite her distress over Charles Manderley's visit, Mrs Budley felt she should have been more vehement in her suspicions about the cook.

The marquess was drawing on his driving gloves preparatory to going out when his butler arrived to inform him that Sir Philip Sommerville wished to see him.

'Put him in the library,' said the marquess. His first

140

worrying thought was that something had happened to Mrs Budley, or he would not have received Sir Philip, to whom he had taken a dislike.

He eyed the small figure of Sir Philip as he eventually entered his library, thinking what an old horror the man was.

He executed a bow. 'Your servant, Sir Philip. What is the reason for your call?'

'Mrs Budley,' replied Sir Philip.

The marquess sat down suddenly, his heart lurching. 'What has happened? What is wrong?'

'Only that one of your garrulous friends has seen fit to insult her. She does not have parents or family to protect her. Mr Manderley called on her and told her you were all set to marry a Miss Arnold and that Mrs Budley by pursuing you was ruining your reputation.'

The marquess's face went quite stiff with distaste. He damned Charles in his heart. But he said, 'I can only apologize for the behaviour of my friend. Such a thing will not happen again.'

'Mr Manderley, it appears, did have certain grounds for gossip, although it strikes me that Mrs Budley is the pursued and you the pursuer, my lord.'

'Mrs Budley and I are friends. Now, if you will excuse me—'

'I don't go around giving females passionate kisses and then calling 'em friends,' said Sir Philip with a horrible leer – second-best teeth, wooden ones, exposed in all their glory. 'What about the Hitchcocks's ball?'

'As I said, I am busy, and—'

'No, you don't, my lord.' Sir Philip pointed at the

marquess with his cane. 'Just what are your intentions regarding our Mrs Budley?'

'Damn your impertinence!'

'Your intentions, my lord!'

'Friendship.'

'Then may I suggest that you behave like a friend and have a mind to her reputation.' Sir Philip's old eyes flashed with contempt. 'You fancy her but you haven't the guts to court her. So you'll wed some milk-and-water miss and be heartily bored for the rest of your life and it will serve you right. Don't come calling again, my lord. And don't glare at me. You and your unfortunate choice of friends brought this down on your head. Good day to you!'

And with stiff dignity, Sir Philip walked from the library.

His face grim, the marquess shortly followed him out, but no longer to go to the City to see his agent. He was searching for Charles Manderley and wondering angrily why friends of the battlefield, who had seemed such sterling chaps amidst fear and danger, should appear like overgrown schoolboys in civilian life.

He found Charles Manderley at his lodgings and started without preamble. 'How dare you interfere in my private life? How dare you subject a friend of mine to such crass insult?'

Charles had the grace to blush. But he said defiantly, 'I was worried when I heard the gossip about you.'

'From whom?'

'From Lady Stanton.' Charles did not think it politic to mention Mr Pym.

'From that trollop? I have now learned of *her* reputation. Mrs Budley is a lady of sterling and unblemished character. I have no intention of proposing marriage to Miss Arnold, as you had the infernal cheek to inform her.'

'But think of your family name! You can't go marrying someone in trade!'

'I am not marrying Mrs Budley. I am not, at the moment, marrying anyone. What do I have to do to make you mind your own business? Never go near Mrs Budley again. If you do, Charles, I shall be forced to call you out. I will now call on her myself and try to repair some of the damage.'

But when he entered the Poor Relation, he was met by Lady Fortescue, who had been primed by Sir Philip – a Sir Philip now questioning the staff in the kitchen over the disappearing cook, Despard.

She was very grande dame, very stiffly on her stiffs. She made the marquess feel like a grubby schoolboy.

'Mrs Budley cannot receive you now or at any time in the future,' she said when she had heard his request. 'Ah, Colonel Sandhurst, your arrival is most timely; please escort his lordship to the door.'

So that was that, thought the marquess, rather sadly. Perhaps it was just as well Manderley had brought things to a head. He had no right to put her reputation at risk. He turned in at the doors of Fribourg and Treyer and bought the most expensive flask of perfume in the shop and instructed them to send it to Mrs Budley.

Sir Philip emerged from the kitchen in time to receive it from the perfumier's messenger. He was about to refuse it on Mrs Budley's behalf, but he loved perfume, so he accepted it and took it off to hide it in his own room.

A week later, Despard was sitting in an inn at Dover waiting for a favourable wind. He had papers to say that he was an American, Louis Rossingnole. A bribe to the captain had ensured that although registered as sailing all the way to America, he would in fact leave the ship at Boulogne when it crossed the Channel on the first leg of its journey.

All his elation at the thought of going home had slowly died. He was bored. He missed the excitement of the hotel, where each meal had been for him like a theatrical production. Lord Ager's ball would soon take place, and there would be no Despard to bring glory to the hotel.

Wind drove gusts of rain against the glass of the inn windows and soughed along the narrow streets of Dover with a mournful sound. He decided to go out for a walk down to the harbour, as if by looking out to sea he could calm the waves and bring a wind to bear him home.

Soon he stood gloomily on the glistening rain-washed cobbles and looked at the masts of the shipping, heeling and dancing wildly at anchor like some Birnam Wood about to advance on Dunsinane.

'It's you, Despard, isn't it?' said a voice at his ear.

Because of the tumult of the wind and waves, and the creaking of ships' timbers, he had not heard anyone approach and let out a gasp of fright and reached in his pocket for his gun.

'It's me, Duvalier,' said the man.

Despard peered in the gloom at the man confronting him. 'Duvalier!' he said in a wondering voice. Duvalier, who had been his childhood friend and neighbour in Paris. Duvalier, here, in England.

'What are you doing here?' asked Despard.

'I come here sometimes,' said Duvalier, 'to look out to sea. I am working here, at the Pelican, as a scullion.'

'Why? Why are you not fighting for Napoleon?'

'I am saving my neck, my friend. I heard news I was next for the guillotine, and so I fled.'

'But you are not an aristocrat. Why should they cut off your head?'

Duvalier gave a bitter laugh. 'How long have you been away? Someone has only to inform against you. Some man owed me money. He could not pay. So he went to the authorities and said I was a spy for the English. My days were numbered.'

'Let us go somewhere out of this cruel wind,' said Despard urgently.

They found a quiet tavern in a back street and a shadowy corner. They lowered their voices so that the few other people in the tap would not hear that they spoke in French.

Despard outlined briefly what had happened to him. 'But my luck has turned,' he said. 'I will set up my own restaurant in France with my old friend, Rougement.'

'Rougement's dead.'

'How? When? Why?'

'Two years ago. Guillotined. He had been taken prisoner by the English. He escaped and made his way back to France, to Paris. He was tried as a deserter and found guilty and guillotined. Do not go back, my friend, or it will be the worse for you.'

'But what are we fighting for? For liberty and equality.'

'Doesn't exist,' said Duvalier with a shrug.

'But you were a good chef. What are these barbarians doing employing you as a scullion?'

'All they want here is their roast beef. I am here on sufferance. I report regularly to the authorities. I live quietly but I stay alive.'

Despard sat in silence, his dreams falling about him. At the Poor Relation, he had been a *name*. He now realized his predicament if he went home. Why had he not made his escape before instead of working for the *sale Anglais*? But he had money and papers. He could go to America. But all at once he wanted to go home, and home was the hotel in Bond Street.

A furious Sir Philip might call the authorities. But how could he do that, thought Despard, for the first time, without implicating himself, without confessing that he had been knowingly harbouring an escaped prisoner? But he could, came the next dismal thought. Sir Philip was an expert liar. Despard could hear him now. 'You would take the word of a Frenchman and not *mine*.'

He shifted in his seat and the letter implicating herself that Lady Stanton had given him crackled in his pocket.

A slow smile crossed his twisted features. Sir Philip would forgive all to get his hands on such a letter.

He looked at Duvalier. 'How would you like to return to London and work for me in a grand hotel in the West End, frequented by all the nobility?'

'But I would need to explain to the authorities here where I was going and they would wish to see you.'

'I have false papers. You can use them. You are now Louis Rossignole, an American. Think on it, my friend. We combine our cooking talents and London will never have tasted anything like it!'

EIGHT

The cook was a good cook, as cooks go;
and as cooks go she went.

SAKI

As Sir Philip was to say long afterwards, Mrs Budley
might have achieved some of Despard's greatness,
given another year, but with Lord Ager's ball hard
upon them, it seemed as if their reputation for top
cuisine was gone forever.

Such dishes as appeared in the dining room of the
hotel were good, and some of the sauces were
excellent, but Mrs Budley was not capable of creating
dishes that would be talked about for long afterwards
and had little knowledge of confectionery, and so there
would be no stunning centre-piece such as the Battle of
Trafalgar, which had so amazed the guests at the
Hitchcocks's ball.

And Mrs Budley was tired. She could never remember being quite so tired before. Not only was the heat of
the kitchen exhausting, but she had to battle perpet-
ually for ascendency over the kitchen staff, who had
begun to relax now that Despard's ferocious temper
and iron rule were no longer around to plague them.

At first she had been buoyed up by the fact that the marquess would not see her at the ball. She would be hidden away in Lord Ager's kitchens. She nursed a little hope that he might miss her, might ask for her. How she wished she had never told the others she could cope. Surely then Sir Philip would have been spurred on to find another French chef and she could appear in her brand-new gown of finest sprigged muslin, made by one of the leading dressmakers. The sensible side of her mind told her that after such a humiliation as had been dealt out to her by Charles Manderley, it was folly to think of the marquess at all, but he had been living inside her head, inside her dreams, for so long that it was hard to banish him.

Gossip had reached Lord Ager that the Poor Relation's famous chef had deserted the hotel, gossip busily relayed to his ears by Lady Stanton through her friends. Alarmed, he had demanded to see Despard, but the enterprising Sir Philip had produced an actor.

Lady Stanton, the day before the ball, finally heard that Despard was still at the Poor Relation and she rounded on Jack, the second footman, and demanded that he find out what exactly had happened.

Jack at first planned to simply walk down the area steps to the kitchen door and ask for Despard, but fear and dislike of his mistress sharpened his wits enough to realize that it was in the interests of the hotel to maintain the fiction that Despard was still cook. He changed out of his livery, put on ordinary clothes, and decided to pretend to be delivering potatoes. He went to Covent Garden early in the morning and purchased a sack of potatoes and made his way to Bond Street. He could only hope that the wretched page who might recognize him was nowhere near the hotel kitchen.

He met with a set-back when the door was opened by a scullery maid who stared at him indifferently and said, 'Leave 'em there.'

'Mr Despard always pays me when I deliver,' said Jack quickly. He smiled flirtatiously down at the scullery maid. 'What about a glass of beer for a tired man, bright eyes?'

'Oh, go on with you,' she giggled. 'They don't like strangers in the kitchen. Step into the scullery an' I'll see what I can do.'

Jack stood in the scullery with the sack of potatoes at his feet and listened to the clamour corning from the kitchen. One voice was raised above all the rest, rapping out orders, a female voice, an upper-class voice. Still, that was not so strange in a hotel run by aristocrats.

The little maid came back with a tankard of beer. 'Drink that quickly,' she said.

She was an unprepossessing creature, little more than a dwarf, with a tired grey face and greasy hair, but Jack stopped and kissed her on the cheek and then straightened up and looked down at her with well-feigned admiration. 'Work you hard, does he?' he asked.

'Mrs Budley's a right tyrant,' said the maid.

'Where's that French cook?'

The maid hesitated. They had all been sworn to secrecy. But there could be no harm in a bit of a gossip with this handsome fellow. It was not as if he were some noble's servant or one of the servants from another hotel, only a deliverer of potatoes and equal to her on the social scale.

She giggled and whispered, 'He ran away. Ever such a fuss. We're to pretend he's still here. Silly, if you ask me.'

Jack drained his tankard in one gulp. Time to make his escape.

The scullery door opened and Mrs Budley stood on the threshold.

'Betty, what is this?'

Mrs Budley had gained an air of command. Jack automatically bowed and her eyes narrowed with suspicion.

'Fellow delivering potatoes, mum.'

'We ordered none.' Mrs Budley did not think Jack looked at all like the sort of man who delivered vegetables from Covent Garden.

'He says Mr Despard ordered 'em.'

'When?' demanded Mrs Budley.

'I obey orders for my master,' said Jack. 'That's all.'

'Your master being?'

'Mr Bloggs of Covent Garden,' said Jack.

'Then take these potatoes back to Mr Bloggs and tell him there has been a mistake. Betty, go about your work.'

Mrs Budley stood there while Jack hoisted the potatoes onto his back and made his exit.

She vowed she would go to Covent Garden later and find this Mr Bloggs and see if he existed, but the pressure of work put it out of her mind.

Jack returned triumphant to his ungrateful mistress. She did not reward him, merely nodded and dismissed him.

Now that he no longer adored her, he felt miserable and shabby. All his delight in his livery and his London job faded at last. He found himself longing for the simpler ways of the country.

Lady Stanton held court that afternoon with her little group of friends – Lady Handon, Mrs Tykes-Dunne, Mrs Branston, and Lady Fremley.

'I happen to know,' she said triumphantly, 'that the famous cook, Despard, has quit the Poor Relation and will not be cooking for Lord Ager's ball. They tricked him by saying Despard was still with them. And that creature, Mrs Budley, is to do the catering. What would Lord Ager say to that, I wonder?'

'I would not tell him if I were you,' said Lady Fremley.

'Why not, pray?'

'I cannot but admire this Mrs Budley. There is a certain gallantry in a lady of good birth trying to emulate one of the best chefs London has known.'

'You forget, Lady Fremley, that Mrs Budley is the little wanton who kissed Peterhouse at the Hitchcocks's ball.'

'You forget, Lady Stanton,' said Lady Handon maliciously, 'that it was Peterhouse who kissed Mrs Budley.'

'They deserve to be exposed,' said Mrs Branston hotly. She blamed Mrs Budley for the fact that the marquess no longer asked her daughter to dance.

Lady Stanton smiled slowly. 'They will be, and in the most public manner possible.'

Mrs Budley sat in Lord Ager's kitchen on the following morning and cried her eyes out. As she looked round at the joints of meat, at the piles of produce, and thought that she was expected to cook for two hundred, and not for the twenty or so at the Poor Relation, she realized she could not cope.

At last she dried her eyes and sent the page to find Sir Philip. Gunter's would need to take over the catering, which would cost a fortune, and most of Lord Ager's money would have to be returned.

Not only Sir Philip but Lady Fortescue, Colonel Sandhurst and Miss Tonks came into the kitchen.

'I cannot do it,' wailed Mrs Budley. 'I cannot cope. It is all too much for me. You will need to get Gunter.'

'I happen to know Gunter is catering for the Markham's musicale this evening,' said the colonel. 'What are we to do?'

Miss Tonks sank to her knees. 'Let us pray,' she said.

Suddenly beside himself with rage, Sir Philip kicked the praying Miss Tonks on the backside and sent her sprawling. Colonel Sandhurst seized a carving knife and challenged Sir Philip to a duel. Sir Philip said, 'Gladly,' and seized another carving knife and the two elderly gentlemen began to circle around each other, while Miss Tonks, her balance recovered, prayed on, with her eyes tightly shut.

'Stop it this minute,' shouted Lady Fortescue.

Sir Philip made a savage lunge at the colonel, who dodged it.

'Stop it, I say, or I will never speak to either of you again.' Lady Fortescue's voice rang out over the kitchen.

The colonel promptly put down his knife and Sir Philip began to clean his nails with the point of his, as if that was what he had been planning to do all along.

Lady Fortescue sat down on a kitchen chair and looked about her, the shame-faced colonel, at the still angry Sir Philip, at the praying Miss Tonks, at the red-eyed Mrs Budley.

'Enough is enough,' she said. 'This hotel business is driving us mad. We will explain matters to Lord Ager and salvage what we can. The hotel is a thriving business. We will put it on the market and divide the proceeds and go our separate ways.'

'Look, O Lord, mercifully upon them . . .' intoned Miss Tonks.

Sir Philip sat down suddenly as well. He took off his new black wig and scratched his few remaining hairs. He felt his life was over. Lady Fortescue – Amelia – would no doubt settle in the country with the colonel and there would be no room for him. The colonel would see to that! No more excitement, no more fun. Only a dismal lonely future on his own.

'If Despard were to walk in here, I would kill him,' he said.

And at that moment, Despard walked in, followed by Duvalier, now Rossignole.

Sir Philip picked up the knife again and his eyes blazed with hatred. 'You cur!'

Miss Tonks opened her eyes. 'God heard me,' she exclaimed.

Despard turned to the kitchen staff. 'Get to the servants' hall and stay there until I call you,' he said.

The staff shuffled out. Despard waited until they had gone and then produced Lady Stanton's letter and held it out. 'This will explain all,' he said.

The poor relations crowded around and read the letter. 'You cannot blame me,' said Despard. 'I wanted to go home and would have gone home had not Rossignole here met me at Dover and persuaded me of the folly of it. He, too, is a master chef.'

'Get yourself off,' said Lady Fortescue.

The door to the kitchen opened and Jack walked in with a bag in his hand. Gone was the fashionable sneer. He looked like a large, shuffling country boy.

'I am . . . I was . . .' he said, 'Lady Stanton's footman.'

'The one that tried to ruin my soup!' exclaimed Despard.

'The same,' said Jack wearily. 'But I am come to warn you.'

'Warn us of what?' demanded the colonel.

'I heard my mistress planning to ruin you. She thinks that Despard here is missing. But now I see he is not.'

'What did she plan to do?' asked Sir Philip.

'She plans to wait until the end of the banquet and then suggest Despard be brought upstairs. That way the guests will finally know he had gone. Lord Ager would demand his money back. If Sir Philip produces an actor in Despard's place, she plans to lead the guests to the kitchen to show them that Mrs Budley is the chef.'

'Wait a bit!' Sir Philip's eyes scanned Despard's letter again. 'This letter means we have her.' He rounded on Despard. 'Could you do it, the banquet, I mean?'

Despard shrugged. 'With my friend Rossignole, we will make you the talk of London.'

'Wait a minute,' protested the colonel. A dream had been rising up in his mind's eye of some pretty manor house and marriage to Lady Fortescue. 'This traitor, this villain cannot just walk back into his employ.'

But Lady Fortescue's black eyes had begun to sparkle. 'Then set about it Despard,' she said with all the gaiety of a young girl. 'Mrs Budley, you will stay here this evening, out of sight. You will dress your best and wait outside the door of the supper room. When you hear Lady Stanton make her announcement, you walk in, dressed in your finest. We shall survive.' She laughed. 'And I thought we were finished.'

Miss Tonks hugged Mrs Budley. 'My prayers have been answered.'

Despard ginned and took off his coat and hung it on a nail on the wall.

Jack made for the door.

'Wait!' said Lady Fortescue. 'You have done us a good service. You are a fine upstanding man and we need an ornamental footman to hold open carriage doors. Would you like to be employed by us?'

'Yes,' said Jack simply.

'We will get you a fine livery, but for now you will help Despard. Get to it.'

Only the colonel stood silent. Sometimes he felt ashamed of his longing to be a gentleman again. He fancied a country life with good books in the library and dogs at his heels when he walked round his estate. But to see his beloved Amelia sparkling and happy again gradually raised his spirits and he tucked his dreams away for the moment and followed the others upstairs to supervise the decorating and setting up of the supper room.

Jack was never to forget that long day. He felt he had been plunged into a hell of chaos as the fire roared and the spit turned and the menservants gradually stripped to the waist, labouring like demons in the suffocating heat.

The day wore on and sauces bubbled and Despard swore and cursed as he and Rossignole filled the air with spun sugar. The centre-piece for dessert was to be the Battle of Arroyo Dos Molinos, a little town among the clouds of the Sierra de Montaches in Spain where Rowland Hill, at the head of three thousand British, four thousand Portuguese infantry and four hundred cavalry, had driven out the French. One by one the kitchen staff stopped their work as the miracle arose under Despard's and Rossignole's fingers. The high sugar mountains rose up, the little Spanish town complete with houses and streets began to appear. Upset miniature baggage carts, abandoned by the fleeing French, lay in the streets as the sugar Highlanders of the 71st and 92nd sprang to life in Despard's sculpture. Finally it was finished. Despard and Rossignole, seemingly unaware of the irony that their dessert was celebrating a defeat of the French, hugged and kissed each other when it was finished and then solemnly toasted France in Lord Ager's best burgundy.

The marquess dressed with great care for the ball. He lived next door to Lord Ager. He felt he could sense Mrs Budley's very presence through the walls. She seemed to be stamped on his mind. He could conjure up her hair, her eyes, her voice, her walk. He was beginning to feel like a man obsessed. He had found his heart's desire and he could not do anything about it because of the great wall of his pride.

And yet he had found himself of late avoiding Charles Manderley, and no hopeful miss could any longer claim to have caught his attention, for he entertained a different one every week.

But, he thought, as he selected a diamond pin and carefully placed it among the snowy folds of his cravat, if he married her – just suppose that he married her – then he could remove her from London, from the stigma of trade, and forbid her to see any of that hotel lot again. But she wouldn't promise such a thing, and the trouble was, if she did, then he would be disappointed in her.

What was so shocking about being in trade anyway? ran his angry, troubled thoughts. All these mysterious taboos of society surely were better fitted to some South Sea island tribe. He remembered a fellow officer who had fought alongside his men in the filth and the dirt and the carnage, who had tended wounds, tearing up his shirt to make bandages for some foot-soldier, carrying wounded on his back, seemingly unconscious of the blood staining his once fine uniform. And yet that same officer had flown into a passion at the next camp when no scrubbing woman could be found to do his laundry. The marquess had suggested they do their own and the officer had raged that a gentleman *never* did his own laundry. The marquess could see him now in his mind's eye, covered in blood and lice and yet with his face rigid with hauteur.

Mrs Eliza Budley was like a poison seeping through his blood for which there was no cure. It was one thing to learn to live with a painful wound – he had done that many times – but another to live with this hurting, nagging ache inside.

Behind him stood his valet holding his coat. What did Pomfrey think? Was he in love? Had he ever been in love?

'Have you ever been in love, Pomfrey?' he asked, voicing the thought aloud.

'Yes, my lord, but I managed to get over it.'

'You make it sound like smallpox. Why did you not marry her?'

'The lady in question was a mere housemaid, my lord. I could not stoop so low. Furthermore, I would need to have found other employ.'

Even the servants are mad, thought the marquess. We throw happiness away and settle for misery out of fear of losing face. Ridiculous!

Mr Hamlet, the famous jeweller, refused twice to see Sir Philip but eventually caved in, as he could hear that old man's voice raised outside in more vociferous protest.

'I know why you are here, Sir Philip,' said the jeweller, 'and no, I am not lending you any more. It did not promote sales last time.'

'It's your business,' said Sir Philip with startling mildness in one who had been shouting and complaining so recently, 'but I thought your business could only be helped by gaining the custom of the future Marchioness of Peterhouse.'

'And who is this lady?'

'Our Mrs Budley.'

'Go on with you! He ain't going to marry one of your partners.'

'Nutty about her, spoony about her, and what is more, going to drop the handkerchief tonight.'

'Never! You know this for a fact?'

Sir Philip nodded solemnly. He had, two nights ago, sat up late writing out what he knew about the odd relationship between Mrs Budley and the marquess. The marquess had been kept apart from her. He would see her again at the ball, and Sir Philip wanted to make sure that Mrs Budley looked like a princess.

'What had you in mind?' asked Mr Hamlet.

'I want to see her in one of your new tiaras, the pretty ones, not those great heavy things, diamonds and gold; and a diamond necklace and bracelets.'

'You will guarantee that we get her custom when she is wed?'

'On my heart,' said Sir Philip.

'Very well. I'll see what I can do.'

* * *

Lady Stanton was escorted to the ball by Mr Jasper Brackley. He was once more happy with her, for she seemed to have abandoned all interest in Charles Manderley. His happiness, however, was short-lived. She drank a great deal between dances, in fact she could barely seem to keep away from the supper room. Lady Stanton was being made more cheerful through drink and through the non-appearance of Mrs Budley. The fact that the marquess had not asked her, Lady Stanton, to dance, did not trouble her. She would trounce the poor relations and then return to her pursuit of him.

With the exception of Lady Fremley, Lady Stanton's coterie were gossiping busily so that by the time the guests went in to supper, all knew that the poor relations had been lying about the cook, and the only person unaffected by the gossip was the host, Lord Ager, who had actually met the cook in person, and although startled to find the man bore little resemblance to the actor who had been presented to him before as Despard, had tasted a few of the dishes and pronounced each one a miracle.

Lady Stanton drank more heavily as the meal progressed and exclamations of delight and wonder rose about her. She did not have a very good palate herself and contented herself with thinking that the poor relations had managed to get their hands on another chef. Either that, or Mrs Budley had a rare talent as a cook.

The marquess listened with half an ear to the prattling of the young miss he had escorted to the supper room; Mrs Budley was nowhere in sight. She was still in the kitchen, obviously, ruining her looks over the cooking pots, and not thinking of him.

When the doors to the supper room were at last thrown open and the splendid dessert wheeled in, the guests rose from their seats and crowded around like children.

Lady Stanton realized her moment had come.

'We would all like to congratulate Despard, the French chef,' she said loudly. 'Bring him here.'

Mrs Branston, Mrs Tykes-Dunne, and Lady Handon added their voices to hers.

Lady Stanton stood there with a smile of triumph curving her lips.

Most of the guests were standing. She heard a burst of applause from the doorway and then the crowd parted. Despard stood there in fresh cap and apron. Beside him stood Rossignole. And behind them, also in cap and apron, stood her former footman, Jack.

'Look at this,' said a voice at her elbow. Sir Philip spread out her letter, the one she had given to Despard. She looked down at it in horror. 'See you in court,' said Sir Philip with an evil grin.

'What was that?' asked Mr Brackley.

'Nothing,' she said through white lips. Despard had disappeared, the guests were sitting down again.

And then the double doors at the end of the room were thrown open again. Colonel Sandhurst, who had left the room earlier, entered with Mrs Budley on his arm.

The fine muslin gown cut by the hand of a genius

floated about her body. Diamonds sparkled in her hair, at her neck and on her arms.

The Marquess of Peterhouse stood up and walked down the length of the room.

He raised her hand to his lips and said, 'Mrs Budley, will you marry me?'

Her eyes sparkled brighter than her diamonds as she looked up at him and said simply, 'Yes.'

The colonel felt a lump in his throat as he passed Mrs Budley to the marquess, and the pair of them walked out of the supper room together.

They came to a halt in the deserted ballroom.

'It is all so easy, really,' said the marquess, smiling down at her. 'Oh, kiss me, Eliza, and take the pain away.'

He strained her against him and kissed her lips, softly at first, and then with great passion.

They broke apart as the band began to reappear in the gallery above the ballroom. 'A waltz,' called the marquess and then took Mrs Budley in his arms again as the band began to play.

The guests came out of the supper room, whispering and watching as the couple circled dreamily in each other's arms.

The only one missing was Lady Stanton. She had gone home to pack, to escape England and the vengeance of Sir Philip. Charles Manderley looked bemused. That proposal had been overheard and news of it had spread about the supper room. He thought the marquess was behaving disgracefully.

Sir Philip bowed before Lady Fortescue. 'Our dance, I think,' he said.

'We cannot dance here,' protested Lady Fortescue. 'We are the servants.'

'Nothing can spoil our success,' said Sir Philip.

Lady Fortescue smiled suddenly and threw the train of her gown over her arm and danced off with Sir Philip, who held her too tightly and whose head only came up to her bust.

'Miss Tonks,' said the colonel, 'will you honour me?'

And Miss Tonks did, dreaming as she floated around that she was not dancing with the poor old colonel but with some handsome guardsman.

Then there was a commotion at the doorway and the guests stopped dancing and shuffled into two lines. The Prince Regent had arrived.

The poor relations, mindful of their position, stood against the wall, except Mrs Budley. The marquess would not let her escape, holding her hand in a tight clasp as the royal personage moved down the line.

'Tol rol, Peterhouse,' said the prince. 'And who is this dasher?'

'My affianced bride, Mrs Eliza Budley, Your Highness.'

'Vastly pretty. Invite me to the wedding, hey!'

The prince moved on, declaring at the end of the line that he was hungry.

Despard and Rossignole, who were having their own supper in the kitchen, shot to their feet when Sir Philip burst into the kitchen with the news that they had to prepare supper for the Prince Regent.

But Mrs Budley was not around to see the end of the dramatic evening or how the prince had praised his supper to the skies.

She had turned her back on yet another convention and had gone next door with the marquess to his home and was lying in his arms on the sofa in front of the library fire, being kissed and caressed to her heart's content.

She had removed her tiara and it lay on a side table, sparkling in the candlelight.

'We will be married in Warwick,' he murmured against her soft hair. 'Prinny won't travel that far, but we shall survive without him.'

She twisted her head and smiled into his eyes. 'When?'

'As soon as I can arrange a special licence.'

'But my friends will not be able to leave the hotel to be at my wedding.'

'They may visit us. Kiss me again. You are not going to postpone the wedding. We have already wasted so much time.'

She kissed him, but seeming almost flustered and surprised at her own passion, betraying to him that she had never been in love before.

He slid a hand inside her gown and gently caressed her breasts and she shivered with pleasure, remembering with an irrational stab of disloyalty how she had hated her husband's fondling her breasts, for he had kneeded them like dough.

'I am forgetting myself,' he said reluctantly. 'I had better return you to that hotel. It won't be for long. We will soon be married.'

'Married,' echoed Mrs Budley with a happy sigh and turned her lips to his again.

NINE

O fat white woman whom nobody loves.
FRANCES CROFTS CORNFORD

Despard had carefully hidden the gold Lady Stanton
had given him behind the bricks in the kitchen wall. He
and Rossignole stayed up late one night to take out the
bricks and then, after the gold had been secreted, to put
the bricks back and replaster the wall. Which was just
as well for them, for on the day after that, Sir Philip,
studying that letter of Lady Stanton's again, realized
that the least the fickle cook could do was to give his
ill-gotten gains to the hotel coffers.

The French chef looked at Sir Philip mournfully,
spread his hands in a Gallic gesture of resignation and
said that, *hélas*, milady had cheated him and had given
him a bag of rocks. Sir Philip, like everyone else, had
heard that Lady Stanton had left England and so could
not confirm this story. On subsequent mornings,
Despard found Sir Philip had been down during the
night, searching every corner, every pot, every crock,
even upended the flour bin in his rage at not finding
that money which he was sure the chef had hidden.

But he was finally distracted from his search by the

news that he was to have the honour of giving Mrs Budley away at her wedding. His triumph at having scored over the colonel was short-lived, for it transpired that Lady Fortescue had decided that the colonel was of more use to her at the hotel than Sir Philip. He was further soured by the intelligence that he was to travel to Warwickshire with Miss Tonks, who was to be bridesmaid.

It was with bad grace that the ill-assorted couple set out. Miss Tonks was actually looking very well in a new modish travelling dress and a smart bonnet. Success – and the hotel *was* a success – had given the spinster a certain sureness of manner and dignity which she had lacked before.

They were to travel in a hired carriage but without any servants. The hotel was so busy that Betty and John, who usually had the luxury of only waiting on the poor relations, had been drafted in to help with the general work.

Lady Fortescue and Colonel Sandhurst came out onto the pavement to wave goodbye to Sir Philip and Miss Tonks. Sir Philip kissed Lady Fortescue's hand and then tried to kiss her cheek, but she was taller than he and by drawing back a step she left him straining a kiss up into the empty air. Sir Philip climbed into the carriage, the door held open by a beaming Jack in splendid new hotel livery, and sat down beside Miss Tonks in as grim a fit of the sulks as he had ever been in. To add to his miseries, he loathed the country and all in it, from cows to dung heaps to yokels, and he began to say so at length, a long litany of complaints, until Miss Tonks remarked acidly it was amazing how people like Sir Philip turned self-pity in their minds into justified indignation, and that he was a pain and a bore. He said, not for the first time, that she was an acidulous dried-up old spinster, and no wonder no man had ever wanted her, and so they both fell into a bitter silence. The first day, they ate their meals in silence, and in the evening, at the inn at which they stopped for the night, went to their respective rooms without exchanging a word.

Sir Philip had drunk too much the night before and slept until noon, much to Miss Tonks's fury, for it meant they were forced to make a late start and not arrive at the castle until sometime close to midnight. She broke her silence to berate Sir Philip, but her fury only put Sir Philip into something approaching a good mood. The day was fine and sunny and Miss Tonks forced herself to forget the obnoxious Sir Philip and admire the countryside, sleepy under a lazy sun.

Neither of them had thought of highwaymen or footpads, for such creatures surely belonged to the dark, to the wild heaths, certainly not among this well-tailored landscape of neat fields, stone walls, and cropped hedges.

They stopped for a country dinner at four in the afternoon, and then later at nine at another inn for supper. They were rolling comfortably towards their destination in the fading light along the Fosse, that straight Roman road which runs from Gloucestershire to Warwickshire, and were climbing slowly up one of that road's many steep hills when suddenly the coach stopped and a voice cried, 'Hold hard or I'll blow your brains out.'

'Highwaymen, damn them,' muttered Sir Philip. 'Let them take what they want, Miss Tonks. Better to stay alive than try to be brave.'

'But we have the wedding presents for dear Eliza,' protested Miss Tonks.

'She'll be happy to have us in one piece and without the presents,' grumbled Sir Philip. 'Curse that coachman and guard. Can't they fire a shot?'

The carriage door was wrenched open and a burly figure stood there. 'Out!' he ordered.

Sir Philip climbed down and helped Miss Tonks to alight. 'Throw your jewellery on the ground,' ordered the highwayman.

'Haven't got any on,' said Sir Philip, who had packed his one precious stick-pin along with his watch.

In the lights of the carriage lamps, their assailant was revealed as one ill-favoured man on foot. The fact that he had not even bothered to conceal his unlovely features filled Sir Philip with alarm. The highwayman probably meant to leave no witnesses behind.

'Get the trunks unstrapped, old man,' said the highwayman, levelling his pistol at Sir Philip.

'Do it yourself,' said Sir Philip. 'You're going to kill us anyway.'

Miss Tonks felt she was standing in some dream.

'Stop,' she heard herself say calmly. 'I have gold in my reticule. I will give it to you.'

She felt inside her reticule and her fingers closed round the small pistol Lady Fortescue had given her.

'Ladies should always be armed,' she remembered Lady Fortescue say, 'this little toy is quite effective.' And her own protest of, 'I don't know how to fire a gun.' And Lady Fortescue laughing and saying, 'It's primed and ready. You simply point and pull the trigger.'

'Are you going to kill us?' she asked, her own voice seeming to come from far away.

'O' course he is,' said Sir Philip. 'He hasn't even bothered to cover his face.'

'Give it to me,' shouted the highwayman.

And so Miss Tonks did. She raised her reticule and pressed the trigger. The report seemed quite deafening. The highwayman stared in surprise and then dropped to the ground, his own gun spinning uselessly away.

Miss Tonks carried her reticule close to the carriage lamp. 'There's a hole burned in it,' she said in a thin voice.

Sir Philip crouched over the highwayman. 'Straight through the heart,' he marvelled. 'Now where's that coachman and guard?'

He searched round the carriage and then along the road, but it was obvious that the coachman and guard had run off, leaving them to their fate.

'Englishmen are grown soft,' he grumbled to Miss Tonks, who was still peering at the damage to her reticule. 'I'll drive. You'd better climb up on the box with me, Miss Tonks. You ain't going to faint? I'll hand it to you. I've never seen such courage in a female, never.'

'I am not going to faint,' she said in a calm clear voice.

She climbed up onto the box. Sir Philip took a pile of carriage rugs out of the coach and threw them up to her. Then he slammed the carriage door and, made energetic by shock, managed to get himself up onto the box and picked up the reins.

He urged the horses forward up the steep hill. At the top they came out of the black shadow of tall hedges. A full moon shone down, silvering the countryside. He reined in the horses and turned to his companion. 'Hey,' he said softly, 'we're alive!' He began to laugh, throwing an arm around Miss Tonks's thin shoulders, and he laughed until he cried.

'Pray drive on, sir,' said Miss Tonks coldly. 'This is no time for mirth.'

He wiped his eyes and eyed her narrowly and then gave her a sharp slap across the face.

'Oh,' she said, and then, 'Oh! Oh! Oh!' And then she began to shake and scream.

'Get it out now,' said Sir Philip, gathering her close. 'There now. My brave Letitia. Philip's here. Faith, I am proud of you.' And he held her tightly, occasionally giving her an impatient shake until her hysterics calmed down to quiet sobbing.

At last she said, 'We left the body on the road.'

'So we did,' said Sir Philip, picking up the reins. 'Best place for it. Otherwise we'd waste hours of time with the authorities. You saved him a nasty death on some gibbet, Miss Tonks, if your Christian soul is worrying you.'

'But what if he didn't mean to kill us?'

'He did.'

'I could have wounded him.'

'And give him a chance to loose his gun on us? I owe you my life, Miss Tonks.'

They drove on down the steep hill, Sir Philip occasionally casting anxious little glances at his companion. He would have liked to put a comforting arm around her shoulders, but driving a four-in-hand was taking all his strength and concentration.

Miss Tonks hugged the rugs about her, trying to control bouts of shaking.

At last the castle swam up before them like something out of a medieval romance. Under the portcullises they rolled, over the drawbridge, the way that Mrs Budley had come when she had been sent to rob the marquess.

Sir Philip tried to climb down from the box but fell the last two feet and lay helpless on the ground. Miss Tonks climbed down and stood looking at him. She bent down to try to help him up, but her legs suddenly gave way and she fell on top of him.

The castle door swung open and the marquess strode out, followed by his servants.

'Drunk,' he said, looking down at the couple on the ground. He turned to his servants. 'Carry them in.'

Mrs Budley was roused from a deep sleep with the news that Miss Tonks and Sir Philip had arrived. She dressed hurriedly and ran lightly down the stairs to the great hall.

'My dearest.' The marquess went to her. 'Your friends have had a hair-raising adventure. They were held up by a highwayman, their coachman and guard ran away, and Miss Tonks here shot the highwayman!'

'Letitia!' Mrs Budley went and stood before Miss Tonks's chair in front of the huge fireplace. 'How very brave. But I must get you to bed. How did you come to have a gun? How did you manage to fire it?'

'Lady Fortescue gave it to me just before we left. I don't know how I managed to kill that man. I cannot remember now what I thought, or if I thought at all. I am so glad to be safe,' said Miss Tonks, allowing herself to be helped up. 'I can't quite believe it happened.'

'Owe her my life,' said Sir Philip. 'Who would have thought it! Miss Tonks!' He kissed her on the cheek and gave her a quick hug.

Mrs Budley led her friend out and upstairs to one of the guest bedchambers. Two maids followed. One unpacked Miss Tonks's trunk while the other helped Mrs Budley undress Miss Tonks and get her into bed.

'Would you like me to stay with you, Letitia?' asked Mrs Budley.

'No, Eliza. I think perhaps I shall go to sleep right away. I am so very tired. Sir Philip was amazing kind. Odd, is it not? When one is twenty, one dreams of dashing and handsome young lovers; then, when one is thirty, one dreams of quiet vicars or widowers; and now' – her voice broke on a sob – 'when one is over forty, any man will do.'

'And what do you think that meant?' Mrs Budley asked the marquess over the breakfast table the next morning. 'She cannot possibly be beginning to think of Sir Philip in a romantic light. He is over seventy.'

'I would not pay any attention to anything she said, my love. She was babbling with shock.'

But in the week before the wedding, it became noticeable that Miss Tonks and Sir Philip spent a great deal of time together. They went for drives, they went for walks, they played backgammon and Pope Joan. Miss Tonks gained a vague sort of prettiness, not so much in appearance but in a sort of happy ambience.

The castle was gradually filling up with the marquess's relatives, including Mr George Pym, who appeared to have accepted the forthcoming marriage with bad grace.

It was a fine day for the wedding. White was for virgins, and so Mrs Budley was married in cream satin, and Miss Tonks, resplendent in pink taffeta, with the tip of her long nose pink with excitement to match, declared there had never been a more beautiful bide.

But when the wedding service began, Miss Tonks cried. The marquess was so commanding, so handsome with his dark, brooding good looks, so much the man of her lost dreams, that she could not help feeling very sad that she would never find herself in such a blissful situation.

She recovered at the wedding breakfast. Sir Philip made a speech quite awful in its quota of double entendres and salaciousness, but he had been so kind and friendly to her during the visit that even that did not put her out of charity with him.

The marquess and his new marchioness were rarely to be seen on the following days, and when they were they looked exhausted and happy and stared into each other's eyes, picked at their food, looked into each other's eyes again and, as if at some exchanged telepathic signal, took themselves off to their bed-chamber again.

'Should have bought them a new bed as a present,' said Sir Philip. 'They must have worn that one out.'

'I thought Eliza would have been better company,' complained Miss Tonks. 'What can they find to do up there all day long?' She blushed. 'I mean, there are *limits*.'

'And I think we've reached the limit of our stay,' said Sir Philip. 'Let's go home and see the others.'

They had an amicable journey back in one of the marquess's travelling carriages. Neither seemed to want to rush home and they spent a whole day at a pleasant inn at Chipping Norton, just under thirty miles from the castle.

Miss Tonks began to see a future stretching out before her. It wasn't the one of her dreams, but it included, of all people, Sir Philip Sommerville. They would live somewhere far from London, perhaps Chipping Norton, and she would have companionship and that blessed title of 'Mrs' in front of her name at last.

She no longer had to fear the Runners. The hotel was doing well. Surely Lady Fortescue could be persuaded to sell.

And unaware that she was shortly to look back on

those days in Sir Philip's company with sentimental longing, Miss Tonks smiled and chatted and furnished the house of her dreams in her head right down to the colours of curtains and carpets.

Colonel Sandhurst had decided to use the absence of his rival and Miss Tonks to press his suit with Lady Fortescue. But somehow, fate seemed to be against him. All sorts of minor disasters occurred, from querulous and difficult guests to a genuine kitchen fire. Lady Fortescue leaned more and more on her cane, surprised at how much she missed Miss Tonks and how efficient at hotel organization that spinster had become.

But one blessed evening, when their aristocratic guests were all, down to the last one, out for the evening, the colonel suggested a walk in Hyde Park, where they had first met.

He hired an open carriage to take them there, for the evening was fine. He felt as proud as any young buck as he drove smartly down Bond Street with his hat tilted and his whip held at just the correct angle. In just such a way, he thought, he would drive Lady Fortescue home through the country lanes after they were married, back to that trim manor-house of his dreams where there would be no Sir Philip waiting for them.

Lady Fortescue, her back as stiff and straight as it had been when she was a young girl, glanced out at the passing crowd from under the brim of her bonnet, occasionally nodding to some acquaintance – for trade or no trade, no one dared to cut Lady Fortescue.

The colonel drove into the Park and called his team

to a halt by the very bench where he had first met Lady Fortescue. He jumped down and tethered the horses and then helped Lady Fortescue down and led her to the bench and sat beside her.

'Here we are again,' he said. 'Just where I met you.'

Lady Fortescue smiled at him. 'A momentous day. We never thought we would be owners of the hotel, did we? Ah, but that was Sir Philip who bullied us into it.'

The colonel scowled. He wanted to forget the very existence of Sir Philip.

With great daring, he took her gloved hand in one of his and, emboldened by the fact she did not withdraw it, said, 'Amelia, we are both very tired and I think the time has come to discuss our future. You know, you must know, that I would consider myself honoured above all men if you would become my wife.'

She threw him a roguish look, conjuring up, for one fleeting moment, the ghost of the pretty girl she had once been. But she said seriously, 'I had not considered us quitting the hotel so soon. I must confess the last week has been a taxing one. Paradoxically, the more famous we become, the more autocratic and demanding our guests. It would, I admit, be wonderful to wake up one morning and realize all one needs to do is to turn over and go back to sleep.'

'So what is your answer, my heart?'

'Very nearly yes. But give me one more day to think about it.'

He looked about the Park in a sort of dazed happiness. The new green leaves of the trees were luminous in the setting sun. Only one more day to wait!

He woke the following day with a feeling of excited anticipation that he remembered having when he knew his schooldays were over, that it was his sixteenth birthday, and that he was a man at last.

He dressed with extreme care, almost as if preparing for his wedding. His childlike blue eyes sparkled and he applied his silver-backed brushes to his snowy hair until it shone.

He sensed a new excitement in the hotel as he made his way next door. But he quickly decided that the excitement was not in the hotel but in his heart.

'Lady Fortescue?' he asked Jack. He could not approve of this footman having come to the conclusion that any young man who could so readily carry out one of Lady Stanton's nastier schemes was not to be trusted at any time in the future.

'Her ladyship is in the office.'

The colonel swept off his hat and pushed open the door of the office.

Lady Fortescue rose to meet him, her eyes glowing with such a light that his heart turned over.

'Oh, my dear,' she cried. 'Such news.'

He smiled at her tenderly. 'I take it the answer is yes.'

She looked at him in a puzzled way and then her face cleared. 'Oh, *that*. No, no. Such news. The Prince Regent is to dine here tonight! The pinnacle of our achievement. If only Sir Philip and Miss Tonks could be here to share our success.'

The colonel sat down suddenly, feeling very old and tired.

But game to the last, he said, 'Do you remember what we discussed yesterday in the Park?'

'Ah, yes, but we were overset with fatigue and plagued with complaining guests. Do you not know what this means? We can raise our prices. After tonight's visit, we shall be so fashionable that we can pick and choose our guests. So much to do! New covers for the dining room and those new French table napkins. Do go down and check the wine, for no one has such a good palate as you. So much to see to. This is the happiest day of my life!'

She busted off, her ebony cane left forgotten by the desk. The colonel put his head in his hands. 'Damn this hotel,' he said aloud. 'Damn it to hell!'

For Lady Fortescue, it was indeed an evening to remember. His Highness declared himself pleased with his dinner, pronouncing it 'the best in London', and only the colonel reflected sourly that it would be a miracle indeed if the bill were paid.

The Prince stayed five hours, and when he and his friends finally left, the colonel was exhausted and decided he could not enjoy any 'post-mortem' with his beloved and took himself off to his bed.

Lady Fortescue knew why he was sad and tired, but any guilt she felt over that was outweighed with the glory of the success for the hotel.

Sir Philip and Miss Tonks read about it in the newspapers on the last morning of their journey and all the easygoing friendliness disappeared from Sir Philip as he stared at the reports in mounting fury.

'That pair! Hogging all the glory for themselves,' he raged. 'Why did we waste so much boring time in the countryside?'

Miss Tonks looked hurt. 'I thought we had a pleasant little holiday.'

'You would,' he said nastily. 'Who suggested the idea of this hotel in the first place? I did. Who raised the money to get us started? I did. Let's get on our way. They have some explaining to do.'

It was humiliating, thought poor Miss Tonks, that when you finally settled comfortably for second-best – no, she thought angrily, looking at Sir Philip – *fourth*-best – to find that your choice wasn't interested. And now there would be no Eliza to talk to, to discuss romance with. Lady Fortescue obviously thought any of her, Miss Tonks's, dreams of romance unbecoming.

Back into the suburbs of London: trim villas, side by side with pocket-sized gardens, advertisements for Warren's Blacking. Then the houses became taller, more crowded together, the streets busier, and then Hyde Park Corner with the red brick facade of Ashley House on the one side and the red brick face of St George's Hospital on the other. Through the toll gate and so through to Bond Street.

Miss Tonks, squinting down at the fob-watch on her breast, saw that it was five o'clock, the time they usually gathered for tea in their sitting room. She would have liked to delay the confrontation Sir Philip obviously planned. She would have liked to retire to her own room next door, now all her own and no longer to be shared with Eliza, but a glimmer of hope glued her to Sir Philip's side, a hope that once more he would look on her kindly and say complimentary things.

When they entered the sitting room, Lady Fortescue rose to meet them, a smile of welcome on her thin rouged lips, a smile which faded as she met Sir Philip's blazing eyes.

'How could you entertain the Prince Regent and not send for us?' raged Sir Philip.

'Why should we?' declared the colonel, taking Lady Fortescue's hand in his, a gesture which enraged Sir Philip even more.

'Calmly.' Lady Fortescue sat down again. 'We were not informed of the royal visit until the morning of the day he was to arrive here. We did not know whether you were still with Peterhouse or on your road home. How could we get news to you? Be sensible, I beg you.'

'Is this true?' demanded Sir Philip.

'I am not in the habit of lying,' said Lady Fortescue frostily. She turned to Miss Tonks. 'Make yourself comfortable, my dear. Have a dish of tea and tell us all about the wedding.'

'Pah!' said Sir Philip. 'Pooh!' And he stumped out, crashing the door behind him.

'Oh, dear,' fluttered Miss Tonks in distress. 'Sir Philip is himself again. I should have known it would not last.'

'What would not last?' asked Lady Fortescue.

'Just that Sir Philip was so kind, so companionable. I had thought ... Never mind.' She gave a little sigh. 'I shall tell you all about the wedding and about our adventures on the road.'

The new marchioness looked across the teapot at her husband. 'You didn't tell me,' she exclaimed.

'Tell you what?'

She waved the newspaper at him. 'It says here that Prinny had dinner at the Poor Relation.'

'Oh, that.'

'I would have liked to be there,' she said wistfully, thinking how the place must have buzzed with excitement, how Despard would have been flying about the kitchen like a demon, creating miracles. 'Perhaps when we are next in Town, I can hear all about it. Do we plan to go to London soon?'

The marquess experienced an irrational pang of jealousy. She was his wife now, and those odd friends of hers should no longer matter.

'I thought we would go to Yorkshire first,' he said.

'Yorkshire? Why Yorkshire?'

'I have a house and estates there and it is time I saw both. We shall have a splendid visit. And,' he added quickly, seeing the disappointment in her face, 'we can go straight to London on our return, if you wish.'

'Of course.'

'You do not look too happy about the idea.'

'It's just . . .'

He stood up and raised her to her feet and wrapped his arms around her and began to kiss her with all his heart and soul. Bond Street, the hotel, Lady Fortescue, Colonel Sandhurst, Sir Philip, and Miss Tonks flickered for a moment in her brain and then whirled away before a wave of passion. It was to be a long time before she saw any of them again.

Sir Philip stumped into Hyde Park. He was hurt and furious and in his heart he blamed Miss Tonks for having delayed the journey home, forgetting he had been a willing party to it.

He walked for a long time under the trees until his rumbling stomach told him he was hungry and his old aching legs told him he was tired.

He barely noticed a plump matron strolling past him until a lace handkerchief fluttered to the ground.

He stooped to pick it up and handed it to her.

'Oh, sir,' she said. 'How so very kind you are, to be sure.'

'Not at all, dear lady,' he said with automatic gallantry.

She smiled at him roguishly and he took a closer look at her. She had plump rosy cheeks and small brown eyes. She had an enormous bosom, thrust up so high that two mounds of round flesh peeped over the modest neckline of her gown. 'Perhaps you would be so good, sir, to escort me as far as the gate,' she said. 'I am a poor widow woman and do not like to walk alone.'

'Gladly,' he said, some of his hurt and fury easing under the flirtatious admiration in her eyes.

'Allow me to introduce myself,' he said. 'I am Sir Philip Sommerville.'

'And I am Mrs Mary Budge,' said the widow. 'Lawks! You're *that* Sir Philip.'

'What do you mean?' asked Sir Philip uneasily, thinking of a lifetime of misdemeanours.

'Why, the gentleman what owns that hotel in Bond Street. His Majesty was there t'other night.'

'Ah, yes, my hotel,' said Sir Philip, preening before the open admiration in her eyes.

'How did you ever come to think of such an idea, sir? Ever so clever.'

They had reached the gate of the Park. Sir Philip's stomach gave another undignified rumble.

'In fact,' said Mrs Budge, 'I would dearly love to hear all about it. Perhaps I could beg you to share my modest supper.'

Sir Philip was glad of an opportunity to stay away from the others.

He cheerfully accepted. She said she lived in South Audley Street, but in fact she lived above a mews behind South Audley Street in two little rooms. But once the fire was burning brightly and an excellent meal put on the table, Sir Philip felt at home.

He bragged about how he had started the hotel, omitting to mention that the others were partners in the venture.

She heaved a massive sigh. 'I wish I had met you then, before you picked up them other poor relations.' According to Sir Philip, it was he who had found the others. 'I'm a poor relation myself. Got hardly two pennies to rub together, and that's a fact. Let me refill your glass. It's lovely to entertain a gentleman – a real gentleman – after all this time.'

* * *

By the time the poor relations met over the tea-tray the following day, anxiety about Sir Philip's whereabouts was running high.

'How silly of him to go off in a sulk,' said Lady Fortescue, not for the first time. 'How could we possibly let him know the Prince Regent was coming?'

'Where could he have gone?' fretted Miss Tonks. 'He does not *know* anyone else.'

'He's probably getting drunk at Limmer's, as usual,' said the colonel. 'I'll walk along there, if you like.'

'Oh, would you?' Miss Tonks clasped her hands and looked at him appealingly.

Miss Tonks and Lady Fortescue waited anxiously after the colonel went out. Miss Tonks talked about the wedding, trying to remember everything she had failed to tell Lady Fortescue the day before, but after a while it became evident to her that Lady Fortescue wasn't listening and so she fell silent and both women stared at the door.

At last the colonel returned and sat down heavily. He shook his head. 'No one has seen him. There was that fellow, Manderley, there with Mr Pym, both just returned from Warwick, and both cut me. Probably think we all conspired to entrap the marquess for Mrs Budley.'

'I hear something,' cried Miss Tonks. And sure enough, they could hear the sound of Sir Philip's voice as he mounted the stairs.

Miss Tonks ran and opened the door and then stood back with a look of relief which changed rapidly to one of consternation and dismay.

Sir Philip walked into the room leading Mrs Mary Budge by the hand.

He introduced her proudly all round and then said, 'We are five again. I have asked Mrs Budge to join us.'

'Ever so pleased to meet you,' said Mrs Budge. 'Phil was just saying as how we should all get along champion.'

Miss Tonks, thought the colonel, seemed to be fading by the minute back into the dejected spinster she had been when they had first found her. Lady Fortescue's face was a mask of hauteur.

The colonel found his voice. 'And where is this lady to reside? All our rooms are full.'

'She can share with Miss Tonks,' said Sir Philip.

'Oh, no, she can't,' said Miss Tonks. 'No, no, no!'

'Mrs Budge can have my room and I'll move in with the colonel,' said Sir Philip.

'Not in a hundred years,' snapped the colonel.

'Well, what about you, Lady Fortescue?'

Lady Fortescue's black eyes flashed. 'Have you run mad?'

The colonel noticed that Mrs Budge seemed quite untroubled by this lack of welcome. A smile creased her fat face. She looked as composed and serene as an Eastern idol.

'I'll find something, my love,' said Sir Philip, patting Mrs Budge's plump hand.

Lady Fortescue rose to her feet. 'Perhaps you would be so good as to wait downstairs in the hall, Mrs Budge. We have some business matters to discuss with Sir Philip.'

'Don't be too long,' said Mrs Budge, lumbering to her feet and patting Sir Philip's cheek.

They waited until they heard her heavy bulk descending the stairs.

'That common fishwife is not staying with us,' said Lady Fortescue. 'Get rid of her.'

'She's a decent lady and I say she stays,' said Sir Philip.

Lady Fortescue looked down her nose and then pronounced, 'Either she goes, *Phil*, or I do.'

Sir Philip leaned back in his chair and clasped his little white hands together and surveyed the three outraged partners over them. 'Look,' he said in a conciliating voice, 'so she's a bit common, but she's got bottom.'

'We couldn't avoid noticing that,' said Miss Tonks with a rare flash of vulgarity. 'It's enormous.'

Sir Philip kept his eyes on Lady Fortescue. 'See here,' he wheedled, 'humour me for a few days and see how she goes. We need extra help, and she's a willing helper. That sitting room in the apartment next door, we never use it. Could put her there for a bit. She says she's got a tidy nest-egg she's prepared to turn over to us. Bit rough round the edges, but good at heart.'

'And good in bed?' asked Lady Fortescue with all the outspoken bluntness of the last century.

Sir Philip grinned.

That was when Miss Tonks slapped his face and ran from the room.

'I think,' said the colonel, 'that you should tell us what you have been up to with Miss Tonks.'

187

'Nothing. What's to get up to with such as Miss Tonks?' demanded Sir Philip. He rose. 'Let Mrs Budge stay. I'll be responsible for her.' He left and the colonel and Lady Fortescue looked at each other.

'Dear lady,' said the colonel, 'surely this is the last straw. You cannot breathe the same air as such a creature. Sell, and come away with me.'

Lady Fortescue's scarlet lips settled into a firm line. 'And have our success snatched away from us because of one fishwife? Never! I will trounce that creature. Your arm, Colonel. It is time to begin the preparations for dinner.'

The colonel did his duty that evening. He waited on society, his courtly head bent over the diners. Society chattered and laughed and whispered and gossiped, waved handkerchiefs and clicked open snuff-boxes. Jewels sent prisms of light flashing about the hotel dining room. Lady Fortescue proudly went from table to table.

It was no longer a hotel dinner but a social event, and to the colonel it seemed as if the guests would never finish and go away.

But at last it was over. He collected his hat and cane and gloves from the office and strode out into Bond Street. He hesitated on the doorstep and then, with a shrug, turned his steps in the direction of Limmer's.

The colonel planned to get well and truly drunk.